BBC CHILDREN'S BOOKS

UK | USA | Canada | Ireland | Australia
India | New Zealand | South Africa

BBC Children's Books are published by Puffin Books,
part of the Penguin Random House group of companies
whose addresses can be found at global.penguinrandomhouse.com.

www.penguin.co.uk   www.puffin.co.uk   www.ladybird.co.uk

First published 2021

002

Written by Steve Cole. Foreword by Rachel Talalay.
Illustrated by David Buisán, Ryan Quickfall, János Orban, John Ross and James Offredi
Text design by Kate Ford at Dynamo Limited
Copyright © BBC, 2021

The moral right of the authors, illustrator and copyright holders has been asserted

BBC, DOCTOR WHO, TARDIS, DALEK, CYBERMAN and K-9 (word marks and logos) are trade marks of the
British Broadcasting Corporation and are used under licence. BBC logo © BBC 1996. Doctor Who logo © BBC
2018. Dalek image © BBC/Terry Nation 1963. Cyberman image © BBC/Kit Pedler/Gerry Davis 1966.
K-9 image © BBC/Bob Baker/Dave Martin 1977. Licensed by BBC Studios.

Printed in Dubai

The authorized representative in the EEA is Penguin Random House Ireland,
Morrison Chambers, 32 Nassau Street, Dublin DO2 YH68

A CIP catalogue record for this book is available from the British Library

ISBN: 978–1–405–94649–0

All correspondence to:
BBC Children's Books
Penguin Random House Children's UK
One Embassy Gardens, 8 Viaduct Gardens
London SW11 7BW

BBC
DOCTOR WHO
ATLAS

JOURNEY THROUGH THE WORLDS
OF THE DOCTOR

PUFFIN

FOREWORD

We are told: dare to dream. Of escapes. Faraway places. Infinite possibilities. But when I was growing up, I was also astonished that many of my dreams were impossible – sometimes they were impractical or too fanciful; other times it was simply because I was a girl and 'girls don't do that'.

I dreamed anyway, but never strayed too far. Well, not until I discovered the infinite joy of *Doctor Who* and was transported through time and space – through universes all the way to the last second of time – and back, through galaxies afar and history unfolding.

I was lucky to have British parents living in the United States. Our trips to England meant new experiences – from scones to Harrods' Way-In, and included discovering Classic Who. My love for Who started then, but grew when the show returned in 2005. I introduced my children to New Who, and they hid their eyes from the new and old monsters and couldn't be torn away.

Daleks. Cybermen. The Silence. Angel statues that killed if you blinked. And on and on.

So I added working on the show to my list of dreams. Obstacles were thrown up: very few women had directed the show and no Americans (or even half-Americans – male or female). But I didn't give up, because the Doctor was calling. When I finally convinced the producers to hire me, I was determined to make the best *Doctor Who* episodes possible. Because the world of *Doctor Who* is epic. And I could be epic. I *had* to be epic. I needed an extra heart and all my imagination and I would depict the epic nature of the show.

As I worked on *Doctor Who* in Cardiff, one of my happy places was sitting outside the Doctor Who Experience and having a sneaky listen to the conversations of the people leaving. Sometimes a kid would be explaining some element of time travel to an adult, or describing a planet or a companion or just how frightened they were of some monster. Other times it was a parent or grandparent explaining the same thing to a kid.

Sometimes it was an argument: who was the best Doctor? Which generation? Which *re*generation? There was bombastic certainty that their opinions were right; that there had never been a Doctor as good as the Fourth or the Seventh or the Tenth or . . .

After I filmed the regeneration of the Twelfth Doctor (Peter Capaldi) to the Thirteenth (Jodie Whittaker) (depending on how you count the War Doctor of course), people would ask me, 'How was Jodie? What kind of Doctor will she be? Does she work?' And I told them, 'Jodie is brilliant,' and, 'Yes, she is the Doctor'– and I reminded them of their

trepidation over every regeneration – what would the next Doctor bring to the role? Part of the joy of *Doctor Who*'s legacy is the fifty-three years (and counting) of these arguments and discussions and strongly held opinions. Yes, the Doctor can be a woman and still be the same beloved, complicated, hero, anti-hero, unforgettable Doctor.

I don't think any other science fiction TV show has had this length, depth or breadth of legacy. When I meet people – especially Americans – who were not fortunate enough to grow up with *Doctor Who*, they are often too frightened to start watching. They throw up obstacles to starting on the journey: 'The world is too complicated; the history too long; I've missed too much.'

Fortunately kids – you kids – have no fear. You won't say, 'The story is too complicated, I don't know what came before'. You are ready now. It doesn't matter where it started; what matters is doing it.

So, get started. Wade right in and experience all of time and space.

This atlas is for all of you. To help you on your journey – beginning, middle or end – and to remind you of the adventures you have taken and loved, lived, cried at or rejoiced with. To entice you on the ones you haven't had yet.

Whenever you can, travel with the Doctor. Inside this book, on your TV or electronic device, in a book or audio edition. Take yourself to these places and create your own new ones. If I hadn't dreamed, or denied the naysayers, I wouldn't be here.

The Doctor is inside this book. The Doctor is outside in the world, waiting to be the hero with two hearts. 'Never cruel. Never cowardly.'

Travel well. The Doctor is waiting.

Rachel Talalay

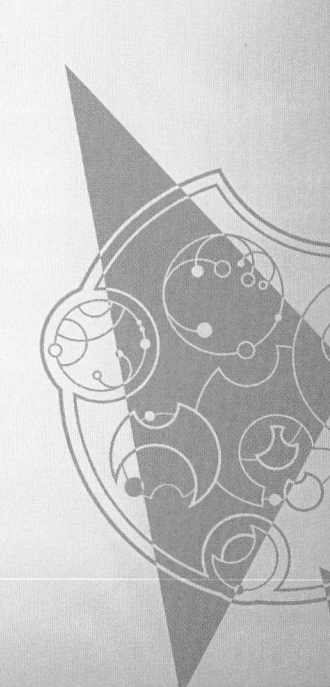

CONTENTS

THE DOCTORS	10
THE DOCTORS COMPANIONS	14
THE TARDIS	18
GALLIFREY	20
THE UNITED KINGDOM	22
PRE-TWENTIETH-CENTURY LONDON	24
TWENTIETH-CENTURY LONDON	26
TWENTY-FIRST-CENTURY LONDON	28
EUROPE	30
THE EAST OF THE EARTH	32
NEW YORK CITY	34
NEW NEW YORK	36
THE AMERICAS	38
VORTIS	40
WAR WORLD	42
TELOS	44

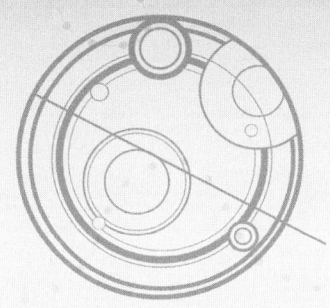
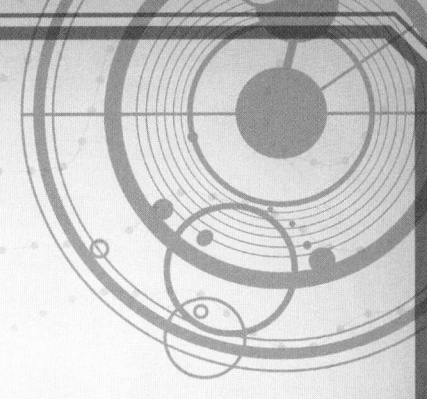

SKARO	46
PLATFORM ONE	48
KROP TOR	50
SATELLITE FIVE / THE GAME STATION	52
TITANIC SPACE LINER	54
MARS	56
THE MOON	58
MARINUS	60
THE MEDUSA CASCADE	62
STARSHIP UK	64
ALFAVA METRAXIS	66
TRENZALORE	68
MONDASIAN COLONY SHIP	70
CONFESSION DIAL	72
DESOLATION	74
ORPHAN 55	76

THE DOCTORS

The Doctor, whose name is known across time and space, is a Time Lord from the planet Gallifrey. With access to time-travel technology and the ability to regenerate, the Time Lords swore only to observe and never to interfere with the events of other planets and species. However, to one Gallifreyan, this proved unbearable. Soon, the Doctor became known as the universe's 'greatest defender'...

THE FIRST DOCTOR

The First Doctor stole a faulty TARDIS to flee Gallifrey with his granddaughter Susan. They soon encountered humans for the first time, and human company softened the Doctor's somewhat self-centred and egotistical nature.

THE SECOND DOCTOR

Younger and more cheerful than his first incarnation, the Second Doctor believed in fighting evil at all costs. His scruffy appearance and tendency to bluster disguised his sharp intellect and iron will, both of which enemies underestimated at their peril.

THE THIRD DOCTOR

Exiled to Earth, the Third Doctor was a self-proclaimed pacifist with a habit of showing off and a passion for gadgets (often designed by him). His quick mind attracted the attention of UNIT, who recruited him as a scientific adviser.

THE FIFTH DOCTOR

Cricket-loving, tea-drinking and mild-mannered, the Fifth Doctor preferred diplomacy to dust-ups. The celery pin on his lapel acted as an alarm to alert him to the presence of praxis gases, to which he was allergic.

THE FOURTH DOCTOR

No longer exiled and now sporting a long, floppy scarf, the Fourth Doctor used his new-found freedom to travel the galaxy. He played the fool to trick his enemies, but his wit and guile were always there, and could be pulled out at any moment (along with a handful of jelly babies!).

THE SIXTH DOCTOR

Unlike his predecessor, the Sixth Doctor was serious, self-absorbed and willing to use physical force. Fearless and armed with the belief that his fate lay in the hands of destiny, he struggled to hold on to his morality as his time drew to a close.

THE SEVENTH DOCTOR

As the question marks on his vest suggest, the Seventh Doctor's curiosity knew no bounds. Although no stranger to manipulating both people and events for what he saw to be 'the greater good', he dedicated himself to traversing the galaxy and putting an end to all evil.

THE EIGHTH DOCTOR

The Eighth Doctor viewed the world with optimistic eyes and a hopeful heart, but the Time War between the Time Lords and the Dalek Empire loomed, and eventually started to take its toll. Despite vowing not to fight, he began to lose hope as each side descended further into darkness.

THE WAR DOCTOR

After being granted four extra minutes of life by the Sisterhood of Karn, the Eighth Doctor chose to regenerate into 'the Warrior'– a version of himself that could bring about the end of the Time War by destroying Gallifrey, the Daleks and even the Time Lords themselves.

THE NINTH DOCTOR

The guilt of his actions in the Last Great Time War weighed heavily on the Ninth Doctor; he struggled with his memories of 'the Warrior'. Moody and full of grief, he believed it was his purpose to save as many lives in the future as his actions had cost in the past.

THE TENTH DOCTOR

With boyish energy, the Tenth Doctor took on Sontarans, werewolves in Scotland and even the Devil himself on Krop Tor. He was fiercely attached to his companions and struggled with loneliness when travelling unaccompanied.

THE DOCTOR'S COMPANIONS

SUSAN, BARBARA AND IAN

Susan, the Doctor's granddaughter, met Ian and Barbara at Coal Hill School in London after fleeing Gallifrey. Together with the First Doctor, they were soon all travelling in the TARDIS, encountering the Voord, the Daleks and even Marco Polo along the way.

VICKI AND STEVEN

After landing in the besieged city of Troy, Vicki fell in love and chose to stay. Steven travelled on with the First Doctor, later settling on the planet of the Elders and the Savages, where he became king.

KATARINA

Katarina began her life as a Trojan handmaid and, after the fall of Troy, travelled with the First Doctor and Steven. She later sacrificed herself to save the Doctor and Steven when a criminal named Kirksen threatened them all.

DODO

Dodo's adventures with the First Doctor began when she mistook the TARDIS for an actual police box. They ended when she was brainwashed by WOTAN, a sentient supercomputer; after being freed by the Doctor, she decided to stay on Earth.

POLLY AND BEN

After helping the First Doctor defeat WOTAN, Polly and Ben joined the Doctor in the TARDIS and later witnessed his regeneration into his second incarnation. After returning to Earth and going their separate ways, they later fell in love and got married.

JAMIE AND VICTORIA

Jamie's travels through time and space began when he met the Second Doctor after the Battle of Culloden, while Victoria's began closer to home – her father accidentally opened a portal to Skaro, where the Daleks held Victoria hostage until the Second Doctor and Jamie rescued her.

ZOE

Aged only sixteen, astrophysicist Zoe Heriot was every bit the Second Doctor's intellectual equal. She travelled with the Doctor and Jamie across the universe, using her knowledge to help them defeat the Cybermen and the Quarks.

THE BRIGADIER

Sir Alistair Gordon Lethbridge-Stewart, or the Brigadier, was a founding member of UNIT. He first met the Doctor in his second incarnation (though he would encounter and accompany him many times). His military background proved invaluable on multiple occasions.

LIZ SHAW

After being recruited to UNIT by the Brigadier, gifted scientist Liz Shaw used her skills to help the Third Doctor fight the Nestene Consciousness, the Silurians and the Primords. Liz later resigned from UNIT and returned to academic life at Cambridge University.

JO GRANT

Strong-minded and determined, Jo Grant began her time with the Third Doctor as his laboratory assistant at UNIT, but became his TARDIS travelling companion when he was freed from exile. After falling in love with environmentalist Clifford Jones, Jo lived a life of activism around the world.

SARAH JANE SMITH

One of the Doctor's most trusted and valued companions, Sarah Jane Smith spent years of her life travelling with the Doctor's third and fourth incarnations after meeting him through UNIT. After leaving the Doctor, she found success in returning to her journalism career.

HARRY SULLIVAN

Meeting the Fourth Doctor only moments after his regeneration, Royal Navy surgeon Harry Sullivan travelled across the universe with the Doctor and Sarah Jane. Harry was brave and capable – he even saved the Doctor's life on Skaro.

LEELA AND K9

The Fourth Doctor first met fierce Leela on her home planet, where she aided him in his fight against Xoanon. Leela jumped at the chance to explore the universe with the Doctor, and along the way they met K9, a robot dog. Leela and K9 eventually settled on Gallifrey.

ROMANA

Like the Doctor, Romana was a Time Lord. She accompanied the Fourth Doctor in his efforts to retrieve the Key to Time and later became the Lady President of the Time Lords of Gallifrey, where she was served by Leela and K9.

ADRIC

After stowing away onboard the TARDIS, Adric became a companion to the fourth and fifth incarnations of the Doctor. He was killed when he was unable to prevent a freighter from crashing into prehistoric Earth as part of a plot by the Cybermen.

NYSSA

Like Zoe and Liz Shaw, Nyssa was a gifted scientist. After her home planet of Traken was destroyed by a wave of entropy, Nyssa journeyed across the universe with the Fourth Doctor and the Fifth Doctor, before settling on Earth with Tegan.

TEGAN

Tegan was enroute to her new job as a flight attendant when she accidentally found herself aboard the TARDIS, and travel of a different kind beckoned! She was a companion of the fourth and fifth incarnations of the Doctor, until she saw the carnage wrought by the Dalek Civil War and decided to leave.

TURLOUGH

Initially recruited by the Black Guardian to assassinate the Fifth Doctor, Vislor Turlough grew fond of the Time Lord after travelling with him. However, when he found his brother, Turlough chose to return with him to their home planet of Trion.

PERI

While Peri enjoyed a warm relationship with the Fifth Doctor, things were not so easy with the Sixth. However, he was upset when he thought Peri had been killed – though he later discovered her death had been faked and she was living happily with King Yrcanos of Thoros Beta.

MEL

A computer genius with a photographic memory, Mel first met the Sixth Doctor when he fought a time demon that was attempting to enter the universe. She travelled with both him and the Seventh Doctor after his regeneration, facing the Rani and the Bannermen along the way.

ACE

Streetwise Ace was fiercely loyal to the Seventh Doctor, whom she called 'Professor'. Born on Earth, she quickly adapted to time–space travel and became the Doctor's trusted companion – even proving herself a weapons whizz by inventing an explosive named 'Nitro-9'.

ROSE

Rose first met the Ninth Doctor when he saved her from the Autons, and before long they were travelling the universe together. Brave and unafraid to speak her mind, Rose cared deeply about the Doctor. When she was dragged into a parallel universe, she was heartbroken to be separated from the Tenth Doctor forever.

CAPTAIN JACK HARKNESS

After first meeting the Ninth Doctor in London during the Blitz, the charming Time Agent Captain Jack Harkness became one of the Tenth Doctor's most trusted allies. When Jack died onboard Satellite Five, Rose revived him – accidentally making him immortal in the process.

MICKEY

Rose's boyfriend Mickey was more interested in the footy results than intergalactic threats, but that all changed when he met the Ninth Doctor. Before too long, Mickey had battled Daleks and Cybermen, and even blown up 10 Downing Street to defeat the Slitheen!

DONNA

The first (and so far only!) companion to enter the TARDIS in a wedding dress, Donna saved all of reality from Davros and his Daleks at the Medusa Cascade, when she accidentally transferred some of the Tenth Doctor's mind into her own to become 'DoctorDonna'.

MARTHA

Dr Martha Jones travelled with the Tenth Doctor, but left when her feelings for him became too intense. However, she wasn't quite done protecting the universe: she later worked at UNIT, Torchwood and as a freelance alien-fighter with her new husband, Mickey.

AMY AND RORY

Amy first met the Eleventh Doctor when she was seven years old and he crash-landed the TARDIS in her garden. The memory of the 'Raggedy Doctor' stayed with her, and years later she seized the chance to join him in the TARDIS, bringing her fiancé, Rory, along too.

RIVER

Born Melody Pond, Amy and Rory's infant daughter was stolen from her parents by Madame Kovarian and reared to kill the Doctor. Known by the name River Song, she apparently killed the Eleventh Doctor at Lake Silencio, and also went on to become the Doctor's wife.

CLARA

After entering the Eleventh Doctor's timeline on Trenzalore, splinters of Clara Oswald were sent back in time to interact with all of his previous incarnations (bar the War Doctor). This led to the Eleventh Doctor labelling her 'the Impossible Girl' and vowing to track her down.

BILL

The Twelfth Doctor saw Bill's potential when they first met, and he asked her to join him. Tragedy struck when she was converted into a Cyberman, but after she was rescued by her crush, Heather, they chose to leave the Doctor and explore the universe together.

NARDOLE

A former black-market trader and con-artist, Nardole was first introduced to the Twelfth Doctor by River Song. Together with the Doctor, he guarded the vault containing Missy at St Luke's University, investigated Harmony Shoal and journeyed on many other adventures.

GRAHAM, RYAN AND YAZ

These three companions already knew each other before joining the Thirteenth Doctor: Ryan and Yaz were school friends, and Graham was married to Ryan's grandmother Grace. But after helping the Doctor defeat threats like giant spiders and the Stenza, the four truly became Team TARDIS.

THE TARDIS

The TARDIS is the Doctor's time-and-space-travel machine, but it's much more than just a spacecraft. It is dimensionally transcendental, far, far bigger on the inside than on the outside, and contains powers and secrets that would astound even the most advanced civilisations.

The TARDIS has a sick-bay for the treatment of illness or injuries. It shifts location regularly, but in the Eleventh Doctor's time it was situated up the stairs, to the left and left again.

The main TARDIS control room has changed appearance many times (the version shown here was used by the Ninth and Tenth Doctors). All the ship's functions can be operated from here.

The power room is linked to the ship's main drives. It contains enough additional reserves of energy to propel the TARDIS outside of normal time and space.

Following a difficult regeneration, Time Lords may have need of the zero room – a therapeutic space isolated from the background interactions of the universe, in which a vulnerable mind can heal.

The wardrobe has got bigger over time as the Doctor has acquired more and more articles of clothing, and it now contains a spiral staircase leading to multiple levels.

According to the Doctor, the second control room is actually the original control room. Given the simplicity of the console, it was perhaps designed for use by pilots new to space–time travel.

There are a number of bedrooms in the residential quarters that can be decorated according to the tastes of the crew. Pictured here are the rooms belonging to Romana and Adric.

The TARDIS has a vast library, with the wisdom of all times and races stored in slightly haphazard order.

The botanical house and gardens contain many rare plants from across the universe – some of them highly dangerous (especially to Sontarans).

The swimming pool – sometimes known as the 'bathroom' – is a place for crew members to exercise and relax. The Seventh Doctor had to jettison a leaky pool but another appeared in the Eleventh Doctor's TARDIS.

The TARDIS is powered by the Eye of Harmony – a star ripped from its orbit and suspended in a permanent state of decay on Gallifrey.

The TARDIS art gallery contains rare pieces from all times and places. Hidden within it is the ancillary power station, which can be used to run defence mechanisms.

Overgrown and ancient, the cloister room is a quiet, secluded part of the TARDIS where crew members can sit and think in peaceful surroundings.

In a small kitchen and dining area stands the TARDIS food machine. It is capable of synthesising any flavour – for instance, by punching in the code J62/L6 you will get bacon and eggs.

The garage contains many forms of terrestrial transport – typically from Earth – used by the Doctor and his companions. It contains scooters, enhanced motorbikes and the Doctor's yellow vintage car, Bessie.

THE UNITED KINGDOM

Perhaps more than any other place on Earth, the TARDIS has shown a preference for the United Kingdom. Unfortunately, this part of the planet has also proved irresistible to alien invaders and other menaces, too! When he was exiled to Earth, the Third Doctor begrudgingly spent some years based here as a scientific adviser to UNIT.

Cwmtaff is a small village in Wales, which in 2020 was home to a large drilling operation that revived a population of Silurians from suspended animation deep underground.

The Welsh capital, Cardiff, is the site of a space–time rift. In 1869, the gaseous Gelth attempted to use it to invade Earth – and in 2006 the Slitheen tried to use it to blow up the planet.

In 2164, Bedfordshire was turned into a vast mineworks by the Daleks, and was protected by their 'vicious guard dog', the Slyther, as they tried to drill down to the planet's core.

In Gloucester, the Thirteenth Doctor was drawn into a life-changing adventure when a Judoon platoon invaded, looking to capture Ruth Clayton – an unknown incarnation of the Doctor.

Heathrow Airport fell prey to alien interference in 1982, when the Master drew a supersonic Concorde aircraft back to prehistoric times as part of his plan to unleash the alien Xeraphin.

Stonehenge, in Wiltshire, is more than just a prehistoric monument. In the second century, when the Romans ruled Britain, it housed the Pandorica, a prison designed to trap and hold the Eleventh Doctor for all time!

In 1966, Gatwick Airport was the base for terrifying alien activities when alien chameleons infested air travel, kidnapping passengers in spaceships disguised as jet planes and stealing their identities.

PRE-TWENTIETH-CENTURY LONDON

London has long been the capital of England, and from the start forces both good and bad have established bases there to influence the country and beyond. Across the centuries, the TARDIS has brought the Doctor and his friends there to face many a threat.

Thirteen Paternoster Row is the home of Madame Vastra (a Silurian), Jenny (a human maid and Vastra's wife) and their butler, Strax (a Sontaran nurse). The trio – known as the Paternoster Gang – have helped the Doctor in his adventures many times.

In 1814, the Twelfth Doctor and Bill attended a frost fair held on the frozen River Thames. They discovered a giant aquatic creature chained to the bottom of the river, with its waste being used as a new kind of fuel by the unscrupulous Lord Sutcliffe.

The sinister Walter Simeon – the vessel for a formless entity known as the Great Intelligence – sought to take over the world using an army of deadly snowmen.

Newly regenerated, the Twelfth Doctor accidentally brought a gigantic *T. rex* to Victorian London. Calmed and contained by sonic lanterns, it was eventually destroyed by the Half-Faced Man.

TWENTIETH-CENTURY LONDON

As the UK's capital city, London has been the target for all manner of invasions and attacks from outer space – and never more so than during its troubled twentieth century . . .

Fearsome flying reptiles, or pterosaurs, were also sighted. The masterminds behind the dinosaur invasion had a secret base at Moorgate station.

'Operation Golden Age' was a conspiracy to clear out 1970s London by bringing dinosaurs to the present day. Terrified Londoners soon fled the city.

In 1966, WOTAN – an intelligent computer built into the Post Office Tower – created an army of robotic War Machines and attempted to take over the capital.

In the 1970s an invading force of Cybermen emerged from the sewers of London, ruthlessly suppressing the hypnotised population and taking control.

A Test cricket match between England and Australia at the Oval was interrupted when the First Doctor landed the TARDIS there by accident while fleeing a Dalek pursuit squad.

In 1941, wartime Prime Minister Winston Churchill hoped to use advanced military robots against the Nazis. He called them Ironsides – but the Doctor knew them to be Daleks!

The goal of Operation Golden Age was to undo human pollution and damage by reversing time around the world and repopulating the Earth with a small number of people.

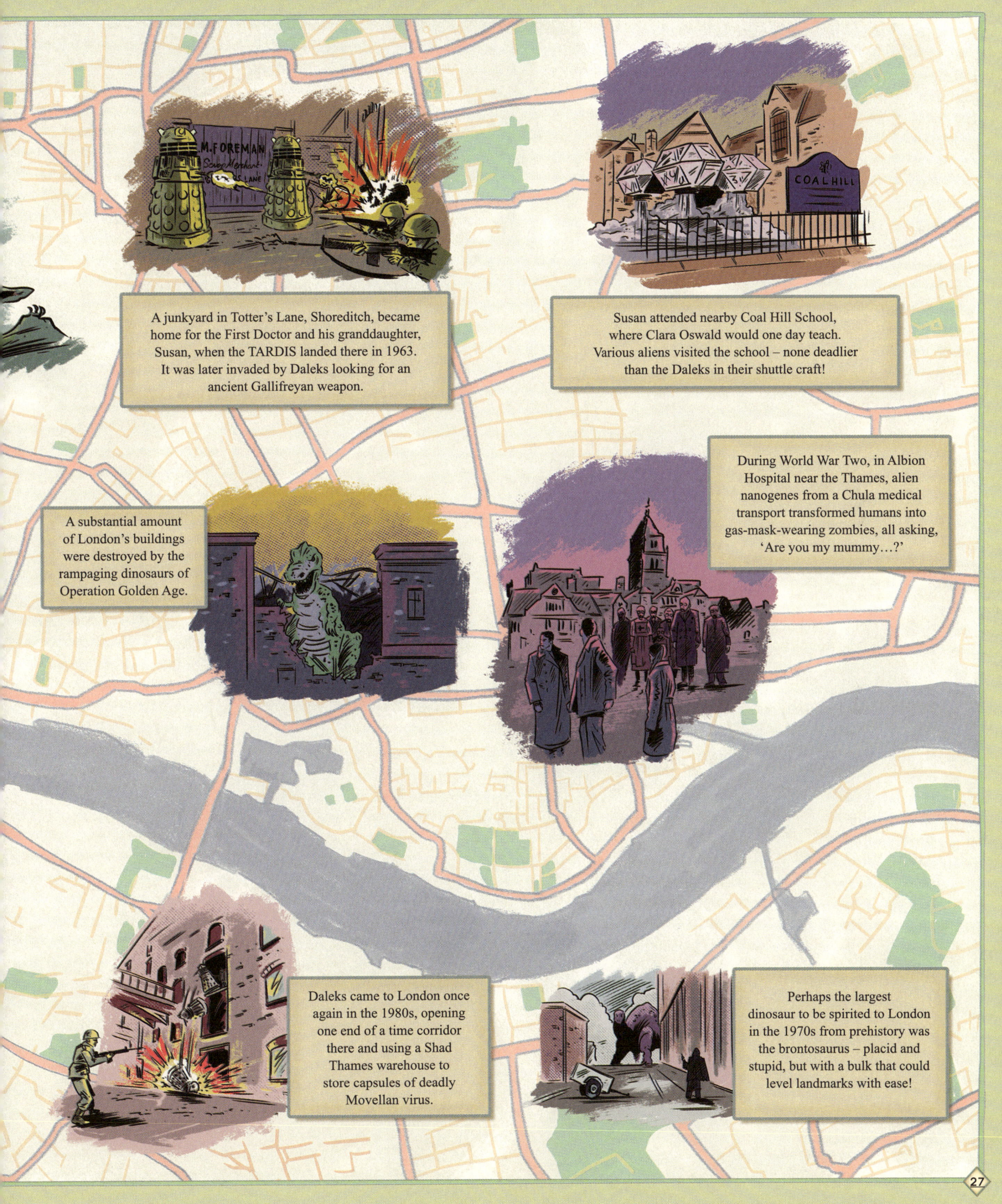

TWENTY-FIRST-CENTURY LONDON

It seems that London will always be a focal point for evil forces and earth-shattering schemes. Certainly the twenty-first century has seen several near-calamities and alien plots faced by different Doctors and their friends – sometimes at a terrible cost . . .

Hidden in Central London by a misdirection circuit is Trap Street, where Mayor Me presided over alien refugees. Here, Clara was tragically 'killed' by a Quantum Shade in the form of a raven.

The painting *Gallifrey Falls No More* is displayed at the National Gallery in Trafalgar Square, and attended by the mysterious Curator who seems to know an awful lot about being the Doctor . . .

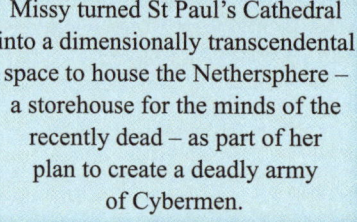

Missy turned St Paul's Cathedral into a dimensionally transcendental space to house the Nethersphere – a storehouse for the minds of the recently dead – as part of her plan to create a deadly army of Cybermen.

The Slitheen infiltrated 10 Downing Street, gaining control of Britain's nuclear weapons, before the Ninth Doctor and Rose managed to stop them.

Elizabeth Tower, which houses the Big Ben bell, was destroyed by a crash-landing spacecraft apparently steered by a space pig – in fact, it was a hoax staged by the evil Slitheen, who wanted to plunge the Earth into World War Three.

The Nestene Consciousness – the hive mind behind the deadly, plastic Autons – built a base beneath the London Eye, and turned the Eye into a massive transmitter that brought the murderous mannequins to life.

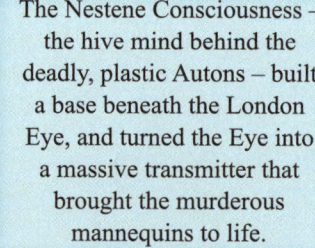

Deffry Vale High School in West London was where the cunning Krillitanes used children's brains and imaginations in an attempt to unlock the secrets of the universe.

The Rattigan Academy in Richmond was formed to advance science and technology – but soon became a front for a Sontaran invasion.

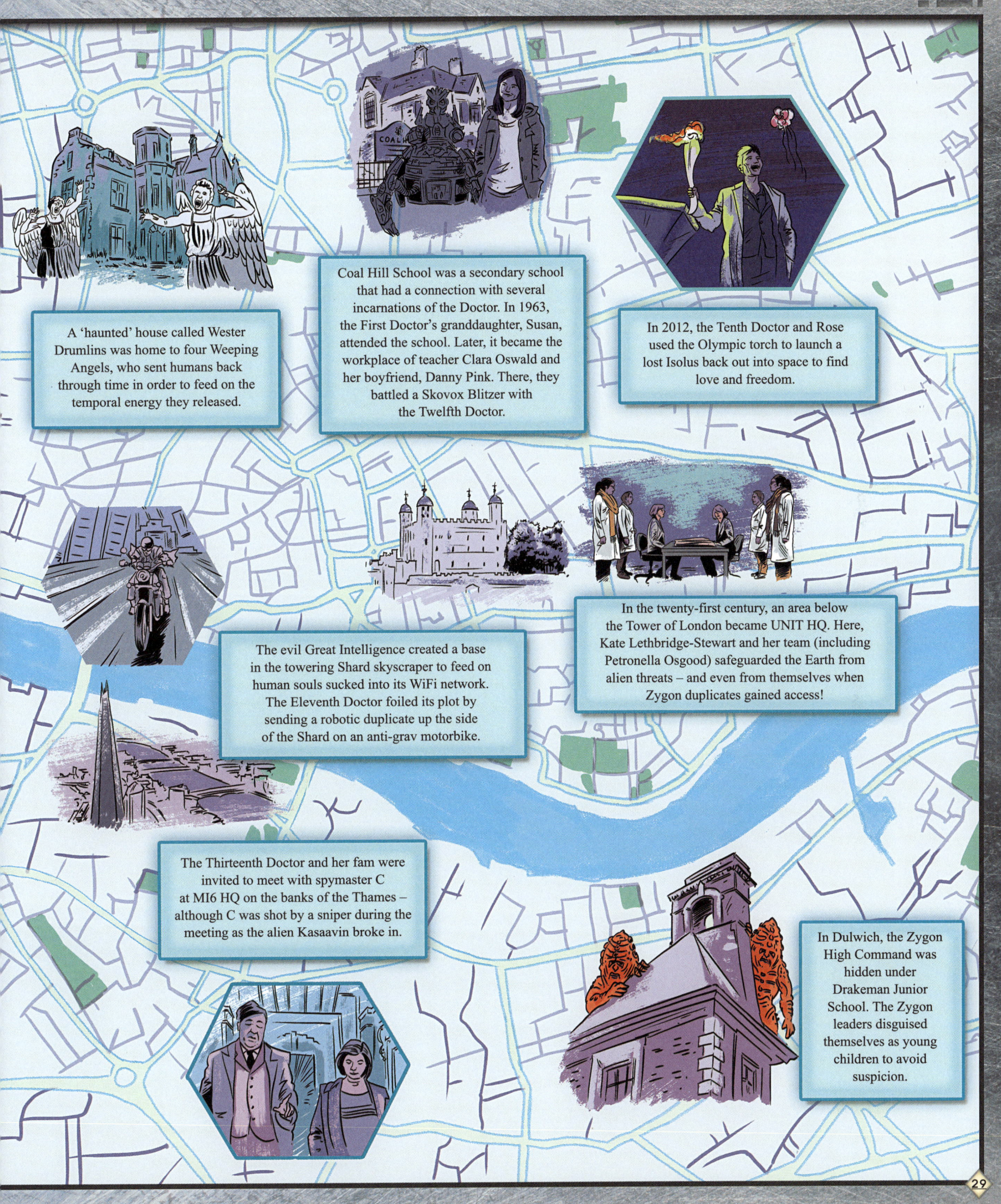

A 'haunted' house called Wester Drumlins was home to four Weeping Angels, who sent humans back through time in order to feed on the temporal energy they released.

Coal Hill School was a secondary school that had a connection with several incarnations of the Doctor. In 1963, the First Doctor's granddaughter, Susan, attended the school. Later, it became the workplace of teacher Clara Oswald and her boyfriend, Danny Pink. There, they battled a Skovox Blitzer with the Twelfth Doctor.

In 2012, the Tenth Doctor and Rose used the Olympic torch to launch a lost Isolus back out into space to find love and freedom.

The evil Great Intelligence created a base in the towering Shard skyscraper to feed on human souls sucked into its WiFi network. The Eleventh Doctor foiled its plot by sending a robotic duplicate up the side of the Shard on an anti-grav motorbike.

In the twenty-first century, an area below the Tower of London became UNIT HQ. Here, Kate Lethbridge-Stewart and her team (including Petronella Osgood) safeguarded the Earth from alien threats – and even from themselves when Zygon duplicates gained access!

The Thirteenth Doctor and her fam were invited to meet with spymaster C at MI6 HQ on the banks of the Thames – although C was shot by a sniper during the meeting as the alien Kasaavin broke in.

In Dulwich, the Zygon High Command was hidden under Drakeman Junior School. The Zygon leaders disguised themselves as young children to avoid suspicion.

29

EUROPE

The United Kingdom seems to be one of the Doctor's favourite stomping grounds, but the TARDIS has taken its crew on many adventures across the English Channel to Britain's near neighbours on Earth.

Amsterdam was located on the curve of the Arc of Infinity, a dimensional gateway. Renegade Time Lord Omega and his bio-synthesised servant the Ergon hid here, planning to use the Arc to escape their anti-matter universe.

IRELAND

UNITED KINGDOM

In Auvers-sur-Oise, France, the Eleventh Doctor met troubled painter Vincent van Gogh – as well as a wounded alien omnivore, the Krafayis.

AMSTERDAM

In 1699, off the coast of Portugal, Captain Avery and the crew of his ship, the *Fancy*, encountered the sinister Siren – who was in fact a virtual doctor from a trapped alien craft.

Paris was also where the Fourth Doctor encountered Scaroth – last of the Jagaroth, a warlike alien race. The evil Scaroth wanted to travel back in time and change history – saving his spacecraft but destroying life on Earth.

PARIS •

In Paris during World War Two, the Thirteenth Doctor confronted her arch-enemy, the Master – who was disguised as a Nazi officer – atop the Eiffel Tower.

FRANCE

NORTH ATLANTIC OCEAN

SPAIN

• SEVILLE

Seville, Spain, was used as a hideaway for a genetic scientist from the future and his Androgum assistants, seeking to grant primitive time travel to the Sontaran race.

PORTUGAL

In eighteenth-century Versailles, the Tenth Doctor came up against repair droids powered by clockwork, who were hunting for the brain of French courtesan Madame de Pompadour.

In the late twentieth century on the volcanic island Lanzarote, an alien beacon was discovered. It was marked with the Misos Triangle, a symbol the Fifth Doctor's companion, Turlough, recognised from his own planet.

ALGERIA

MOROCCO

SWEDEN

FINLAND

NORWAY

In 2018 Norway, the Thirteenth Doctor discovered a portal between Earth and another reality. The Doctor, Yaz and Graham encountered the sinister Ribbons in an anti-zone that kept the two realms apart.

DENMARK

BERLIN

In Nazi Berlin in 1938, the Eleventh Doctor had a fantastic adventure involving the Teselecta – a shape-shifting humanoid starship – and a brush with Adolf Hitler.

POLAND

GERMANY

Sixty miles outside Nuremburg lies Osterhagen Station One – one of several top-secret outposts that can self-destruct the Earth in case of alien invasion, and visited by Martha Jones.

NUREMBERG

AUSTRIA

VENICE

SAN MARTINO

The Eleventh Doctor defeated the Saturnynes – a race of fishlike alien vampires – in sixteenth-century Venice. They planned to sink the city and create a new habitat for themselves, before the Doctor, Amy and Rory foiled their plan.

ITALY

In San Martino, Italy, the Mandragora Helix plotted to end humanity's development in the fifteenth century by granting deadly energy to the power-hungry astrologer Hieronymous.

POMPEII

GREECE

The Tenth Doctor arrived in Pompeii on the exact day Mount Vesuvius erupted in AD 79.

In Ancient Greece, in 500 BC, the philosopher Bigon and other Greeks were kidnapped by the Urbankan leader Monarch, a creature obsessed with life on Earth – and who plotted to end it!

TUNISIA

THE EAST OF THE EARTH

Earth is a big place, and the TARDIS is drawn to dramatic and devastating events all over the planet. From Egypt to Australia, the Doctor has fought to escape the tide of history and to defeat the enemies of the world.

Turkey is the site of the ancient city of Troy, which was destroyed by the Ancient Greeks. The First Doctor gave the Greeks the idea to hide soldiers inside a wooden horse in order to sneak into the city.

The Zygons had a training camp hidden in the nation of Turmezistan. An ancient pyramid later appeared there, and was used by the Monks to entrap human military forces and orchestrate an invasion of Earth.

The First Doctor met King Richard I of England in twelfth-century Palestine. The king, nicknamed Richard the Lionheart due to his reputation for bravery, was fighting alongside his forces during the Third Crusade to try to reconquer the Holy Land.

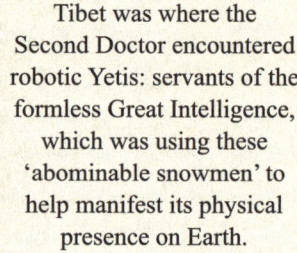

Tibet was where the Second Doctor encountered robotic Yetis: servants of the formless Great Intelligence, which was using these 'abominable snowmen' to help manifest its physical presence on Earth.

During the partition of India in 1947, the Thirteenth Doctor encountered alien assassins called Thijarians in the Punjab region.

Near Cairo, Egypt, lurked the Pyramid of Sutekh – last of the all-powerful Osirans. He was imprisoned for millennia through the power of the Eye of Horus, before the Fourth Doctor stopped him from breaking free to devastate the universe.

In Australia in 2018, the power-mad politician Ramón Salamander conducted successful sun-conservation tests using orbiting satellites – and he happened to look exactly like the Second Doctor!

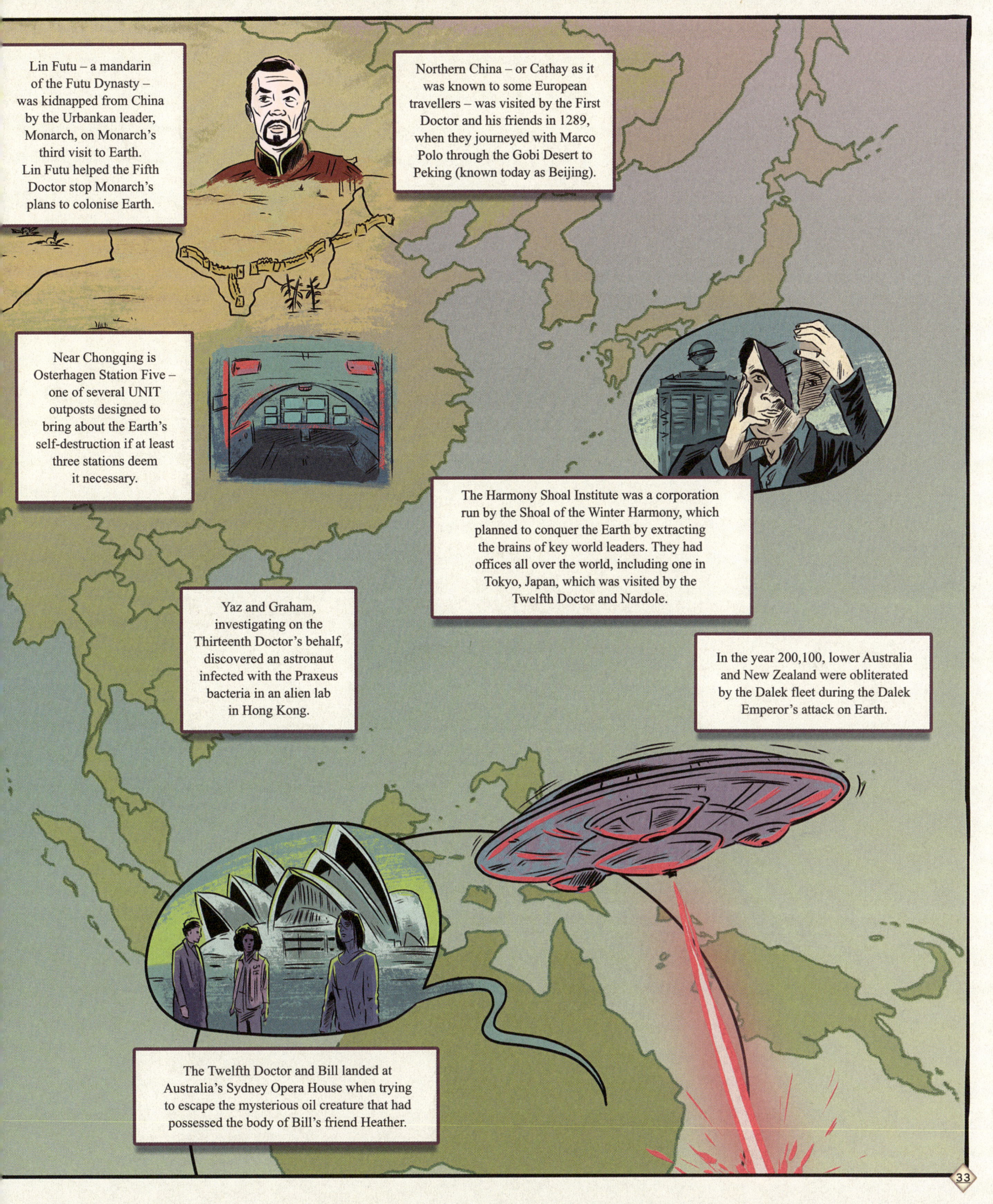

NEW YORK CITY

The TARDIS has landed in New York City, USA, on multiple occasions in the iconic city's hours of need. Some of the deadliest creatures in the universe have attempted to destroy NYC and its world-famous landmarks – but thanks to the Doctor it still stands!

There is a cemetery in Manhattan where Amy's and Rory's gravestones can be found. It was here that Amy said goodbye to the Eleventh Doctor and River Song for the last time.

In 1930, a singer named Tallulah was the star of the show in the New York Revue at the Laurenzi Theater. Her boyfriend, Laszlo, was a stagehand, but danger lurked nearby and one day Laszlo disappeared . . .

In Central Park in 1930 stood Hooverville – a shanty town of huts for people caught in the poverty of the Great Depression. The Tenth Doctor and Martha discovered that many of its residents were being converted into pig slaves or killed by the Daleks.

In 1938, 406 94th Street in Manhattan was home to crime boss Julius Grayle. Alongside his criminal activities, Grayle also collected expensive, unusual artefacts – including a Weeping Angel and several Weeping Cherubs!

Meanwhile, in 2012, the Eleventh Doctor, Amy and Rory enjoyed a picnic in Central Park – not realising it would be their last happy time together . . .

In 1903, New York City was invaded by the Skithra – a race of savage space scavengers resembling giant scorpions and led by a ruthless queen!

Along with the Hooverville residents, New Yorkers like Laszlo were turned into pig slaves by the Daleks and forced to toil for their evil masters in the sewers beneath Manhattan.

In 1966, an American tourist named Morton Dill witnessed the TARDIS materialise on the Empire State Building's observation deck – and was questioned by a pursuing squad of Daleks soon after!

Out on Long Island stood Wardenclyffe Tower, where in the 1900s inventor Nikola Tesla kept his private laboratory. When the Skithra threatened the safety of the world, it was here that Tesla, the Thirteenth Doctor and the fam repelled their attack.

In the Cult of Skaro's genetic laboratory beneath Manhattan, the first human-Dalek – Dalek Sec – masterminded the 'Final Experiment': a way to recreate the Dalek race using humans.

In 1930, the Dalek Cult of Skaro occupied a floor of the newly built Empire State Building in midtown Manhattan. They planned to convert it into a gamma-radiation attractor that would create human-Dalek hybrids, until the Tenth Doctor stopped them.

In order to correct the paradoxes he had created, the Twelfth Doctor set up a 'time-distortion-equaliser thingy' on top of a rooftop in Lower Manhattan. There, he met a boy named Grant, who accidentally ate one of the Doctor's power sources as he thought it was medicine. It gave Grant superpowers, and one day he became the superhero The Ghost.

Near Battery Park stands Winter Quay, an apartment block used by the Weeping Angels in the late 1930s as a battery farm to harvest time energy from human beings.

Winter Quay often received visits from the largest Weeping Angel of all – the one that took over the Statue of Liberty!

At Lake Silencio in Utah in 2011, the Eleventh Doctor was enjoying a picnic with Rory and Amy when an astronaut rose from the lake's waters and shot him dead. It was later revealed to be River Song inside the spacesuit, and the assassination was staged in order to prevent the collapse of time.

The White House in Washington, D.C. is the home of the President of the USA. The Eleventh Doctor went there in 1969, when it was infested with the Silence. A simulation of the Twelfth Doctor went to a virtual version of the White House while investigating the mystery of the Monks.

Elsewhere in Utah, in 2012, the Ninth Doctor and Rose encountered the last surviving Dalek from the Time War – hidden deep beneath the ground in billionaire Henry van Statten's vault.

In 1969, Apollo 11 blasted off for the Moon from the Kennedy Space Center in Florida. The lives of the three astronauts onboard weren't the only thing at stake – the Eleventh Doctor used the mass audience watching on TV to overthrow the Silence's secret rule of Earth.

In 1969, the Eleventh Doctor faked imprisonment in Area 51 – the notorious military base near Dry Springs, Nevada, that contained fallen alien spacecraft.

Separated from the Eleventh Doctor and Amy and on the run from the Silence, Rory was captured by the FBI on Glen Canyon Dam, Arizona.

Drawn by the presence of artron energy, the Thirteenth Doctor, Ryan, Yaz and Graham visited Alabama in 1955 and met civil rights activist Rosa Parks – the target of Krasko, a time-travelling racist and mass murderer.

The Mayan princess Villagra was kidnapped from ancient times by the Urbankan Monarch and preserved in android form on his spaceship. She was told she would rule the Americas following Monarch's eventual invasion.

The First Doctor, Barbara, Ian and Susan visited Mexico in the fifteenth century and became caught up in a violent plot involving the Aztec people.

THE AMERICAS

Though New York appears to be a favourite destination of the TARDIS, the Doctor has also visited many other parts of North America, Central America and South America, encountering friends, foes and unearthly threats across all three . . . .

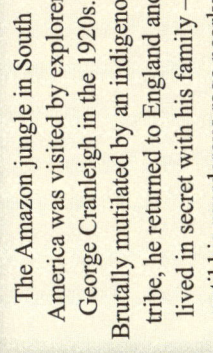

The Amazon jungle in South America was visited by explorer George Cranleigh in the 1920s. Brutally mutilated by an indigenous tribe, he returned to England and lived in secret with his family — until his murderous rage nearly ended the life of the Fifth Doctor's companion Nyssa.

Argentina was the site of Osterhagen Station Two, one of the network of secret doomsday bases that could destroy the Earth in the case of an extreme extraterrestrial emergency.

In Peru, Ryan met Gabriela, the co-host of the video blog Two Girls Roaming. Her co-host Jamila was attacked by birds infected with the Praxeus pathogen, and later died.

San Francisco in 1999 became the site of a world-changing battle between the newly regenerated Eighth Doctor and a resurrected Master, with the entire world at stake!

The First Doctor visited the town of Tombstone, Arizona, in 1881. He and his companions Dodo and Steven became embroiled in the events leading to the infamous gunfight between the Earps and the Clantons at the OK Corral.

WAR WORLD

When the Second Doctor and his companions landed on this nameless planet, they believed they were on the Western Front during World War One. However, the appearance of a soldier who believed it was 1745 made them realise something more sinister was going on. They soon discovered that a mysterious humanoid race known as the War Lords was kidnapping soldiers from different conflicts throughout Earth's history and submitting them to deadly war games…

The War Lords didn't capture soldiers from any conflicts after 1917, as they felt that advancements in military technology on Earth would make the troops a threat to them.

AMERICAN CIVIL WAR ZONE

WORLD WAR ONE WAR ZONE

ENGLISH CIVIL WAR ZONE

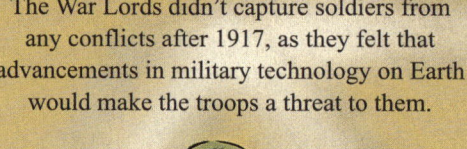

① The War Lords divided the planet into separate zones for each period, making it impossible for the brainwashed soldiers to realise they were no longer on Earth as they continued to fight. The zones were separated by thick mists that humans were unable to pass through.

THIRTY YEARS WAR ZONE

RUSSO–JAPANESE WAR ZONE

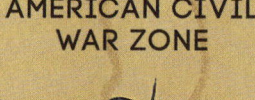

② War Lords disguised as superior officers ran each zone and used hypnotic glasses to control the humans. Special squads of guards were also sent in to keep order if any soldier threatened an uprising in the ranks.

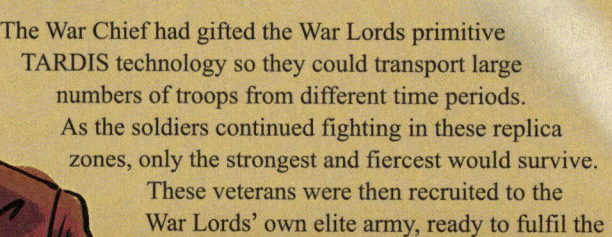

④ The War Chief had gifted the War Lords primitive TARDIS technology so they could transport large numbers of troops from different time periods. As the soldiers continued fighting in these replica zones, only the strongest and fiercest would survive. These veterans were then recruited to the War Lords' own elite army, ready to fulfil the War Lords' plan to conquer the galaxy.

ROMAN ZONE

 After discovering the War Chief and uncovering the War Lords' plan, the Doctor realised that stopping them would take more than just him. For the first time, he appealed to the Time Lords for help by placing a mental message inside a psychic box and transmitting it to Gallifrey.

CRIMEAN WAR ZONE

MEXICAN CIVIL WAR ZONE

③ The war games were controlled from a base in the centre of all the time zones. When the Doctor, Zoe and Jamie infiltrated the base, they found a renegade Time Lord, known as the War Chief, helping the War Lords to build an army of their own.

PENINSULAR WAR ZONE

⑥ The Time Lords heeded the Doctor's plea, and they used their power to kill the War Lords' leader and place the planet under a forcefield. They returned the human survivors to their proper places in time and space, but placed the Doctor on trial under charges of interfering with the affairs of the universe, which they believed was against their code.

BOER WAR ZONE

GREEK ZONE

⑦ The Doctor defended himself by arguing that evil has to be fought, and showed the Time Lords the many monsters he had defeated – Ice Warriors, Yetis, Quarks, Cybermen and, of course, the dreaded Daleks. The Time Lords agreed, but refused to let him go free, instead exiling him to Planet Earth.

43

Beneath the Thal city's protective dome was a great rocket that they used to all but destroy the Kaled race, thereby bringing the Neutronic War to an end.

Handmines were used during the great Thal–Kaled war. The mines rose out of the ground in clusters and surrounded their prey before pulling them beneath the muddy surface to certain death.

As their name suggests, 'Mutos' are mutations, brought about by chemical weapons used by the Thals and Kaleds in their bitter war. The creatures were banished into the wastelands to scavenge like animals.

Inside the Kaleds' research bunker, the Fourth Doctor planned to blow up the Dalek incubator room to stop the Daleks from being created. He just had to touch two wires together . . .

There are many dangers in the swamps of Skaro – Daleks can fall prey to them too!

A colossal Dalek statue towers over the sprawling city below. The Eleventh Doctor was lured to the dome section of the statue, where he was kidnapped by the Daleks.

The Master was once taken to Skaro to face trial for his crimes. He was seemingly executed by the Daleks, but somehow managed to survive their lethal firepower.

The Daleks are a warrior race made up of genetically engineered mutants.

PLATFORM ONE

In the year 5,000,000,000, the Ninth Doctor and Rose visited the alpha-class space station Platform One. It was a viewing platform from which the richest beings in the universe could view a once-in-a-lifetime event – the destruction of the Earth as it was finally engulfed by the fires of the sun . . .

1 Platform One was superbly placed for observing the Earth's demise. Sun filters and tinted glass protected observers from the heat and glare of the planet's destruction.

Intelligent humanoid trees were present, descended from the rainforests of Earth. They were representatives of the Forest of Cheem and led by a treeform named Jabe.

2 The observers of the planet's doom were a curious assortment of the rich and powerful, and they exchanged gifts to mark the momentous occasion. Among them, representing the solicitors Jolco and Jolco, was the Moxx of Balhoon, whose gift was his saliva, which he spat at the other guests.

6 The terrified guests stared through the cracked observation panels as the sun swelled towards them. The Doctor, realising that something was wrong, reprogrammed the spider-bots to find their master, and he uncovered Cassandra's plot.

Mr and Mrs Pakoo were avian humanoids who came for a bird's-eye view of the world's destruction.

7 With only minutes before Platform One was incinerated, the Doctor had to get past some huge rotating fans in order to reach the controls and manually raise the craft's heat shields. The station was saved!

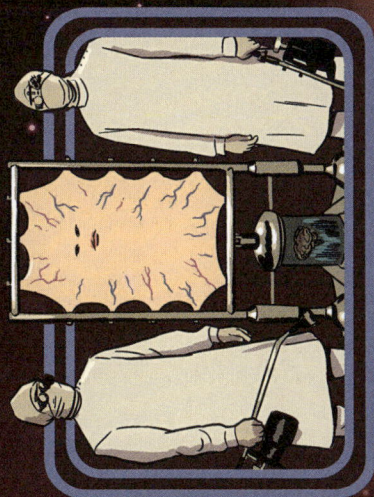

The Brothers Hop Pyleen also came to view the death of Earth. As inventors of the Hyposlip Travel Systems, they were extremely rich and well connected.

Cassandra was not so lucky. With the heat shields around her lowered and her servants teleported elsewhere, she began to dry out and was torn to pieces by the heat. Below her, the sun exploded and destroyed the abandoned planet Earth, much to Rose's dismay.

Also onboard was the Lady Cassandra O'Brien.∆17. She used to be a human being, before more than 700 rounds of plastic surgery left her little more than a layer of skin with eyes and a mouth connected to a brain in a jar below. She came not only to witness the death of her home world, but also with a darker purpose – to sabotage Platform One in order to profit from the deaths of those onboard.

The orbs secretly contained hundreds of spider-bots, which soon infiltrated and deactivated all of the platform's safety features.

The mysterious Adherents of the Repeated Meme were also in attendance, but were in fact androids remotely operated by Cassandra. Their gift to the other attendees was a stainless-steel orb, given as a 'gift of peace in all good faith'.

The Face of Boe, a male Boekind who communicated largely by telepathy, was a sponsor of the observation event. He was one of the oldest beings in the universe.

Ambassadors of the City State of Binding Light were in attendance. Due to their high sensitivity to oxygen, oxygen levels onboard Platform One were monitored at all times.

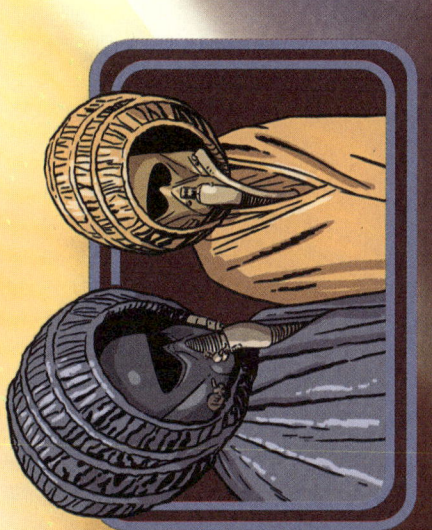

The infinitely famous cybernetic hyperstar Cal 'Spark Plug' MacNannovich joined the party with his partner, Noxwen Van Coofen.

KROP TOR

Orbiting a distant black hole is the barren planet of Krop Tor – the name means 'the Bitter Pill'. According to legend, the black hole was a demon that tried to swallow Krop Tor, but found it was poison and had to spit it out. How could a planet orbit a black hole without being sucked in? A scientific expedition was sent there to learn the truth about this impossible planet, and they soon found out that the legend wasn't far from the truth . . .

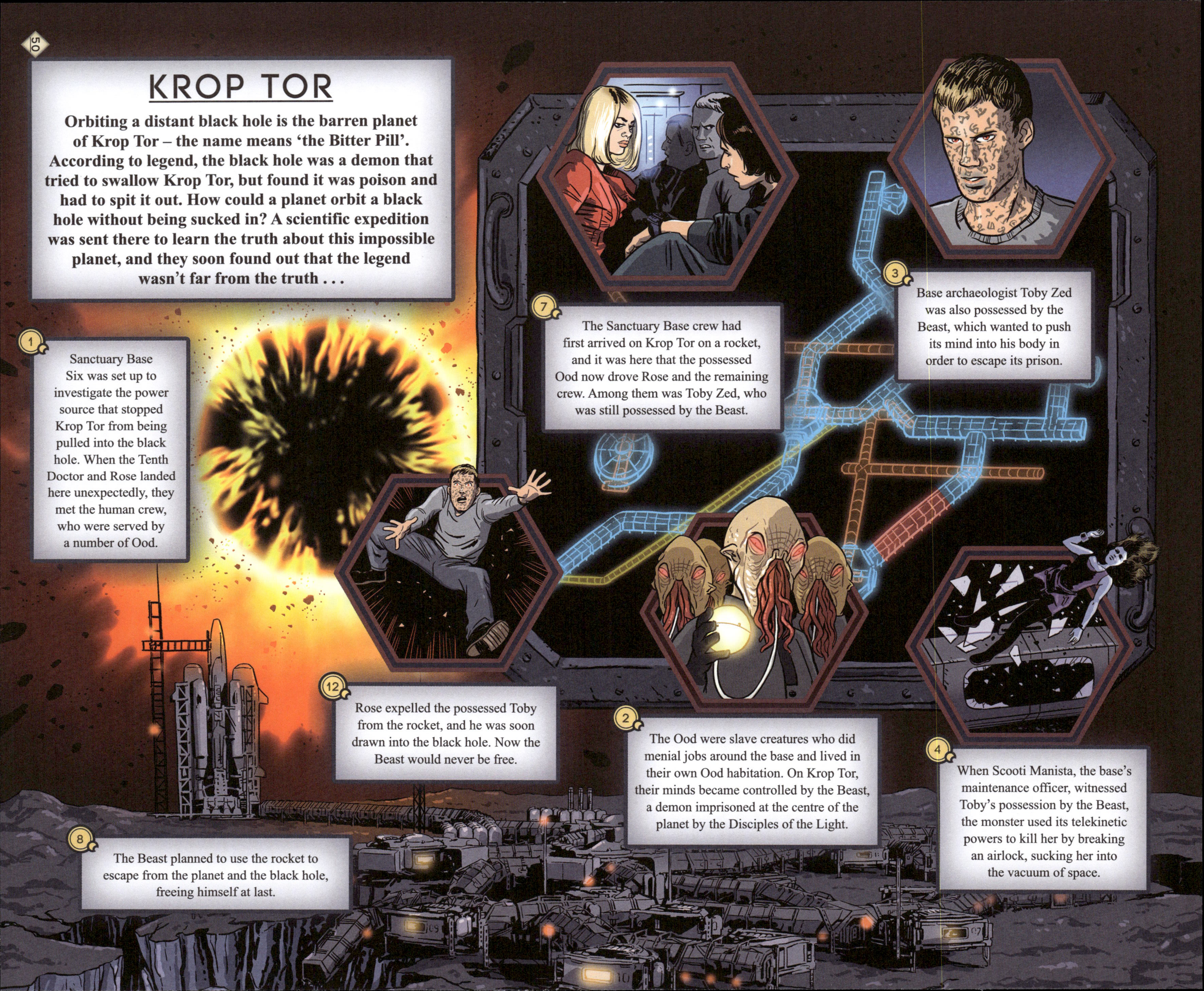

1. Sanctuary Base Six was set up to investigate the power source that stopped Krop Tor from being pulled into the black hole. When the Tenth Doctor and Rose landed here unexpectedly, they met the human crew, who were served by a number of Ood.

2. The Ood were slave creatures who did menial jobs around the base and lived in their own Ood habitation. On Krop Tor, their minds became controlled by the Beast, a demon imprisoned at the centre of the planet by the Disciples of the Light.

3. Base archaeologist Toby Zed was also possessed by the Beast, which wanted to push its mind into his body in order to escape its prison.

4. When Scooti Manista, the base's maintenance officer, witnessed Toby's possession by the Beast, the monster used its telekinetic powers to kill her by breaking an airlock, sucking her into the vacuum of space.

7. The Sanctuary Base crew had first arrived on Krop Tor on a rocket, and it was here that the possessed Ood now drove Rose and the remaining crew. Among them was Toby Zed, who was still possessed by the Beast.

8. The Beast planned to use the rocket to escape from the planet and the black hole, freeing himself at last.

12. Rose expelled the possessed Toby from the rocket, and he was soon drawn into the black hole. Now the Beast would never be free.

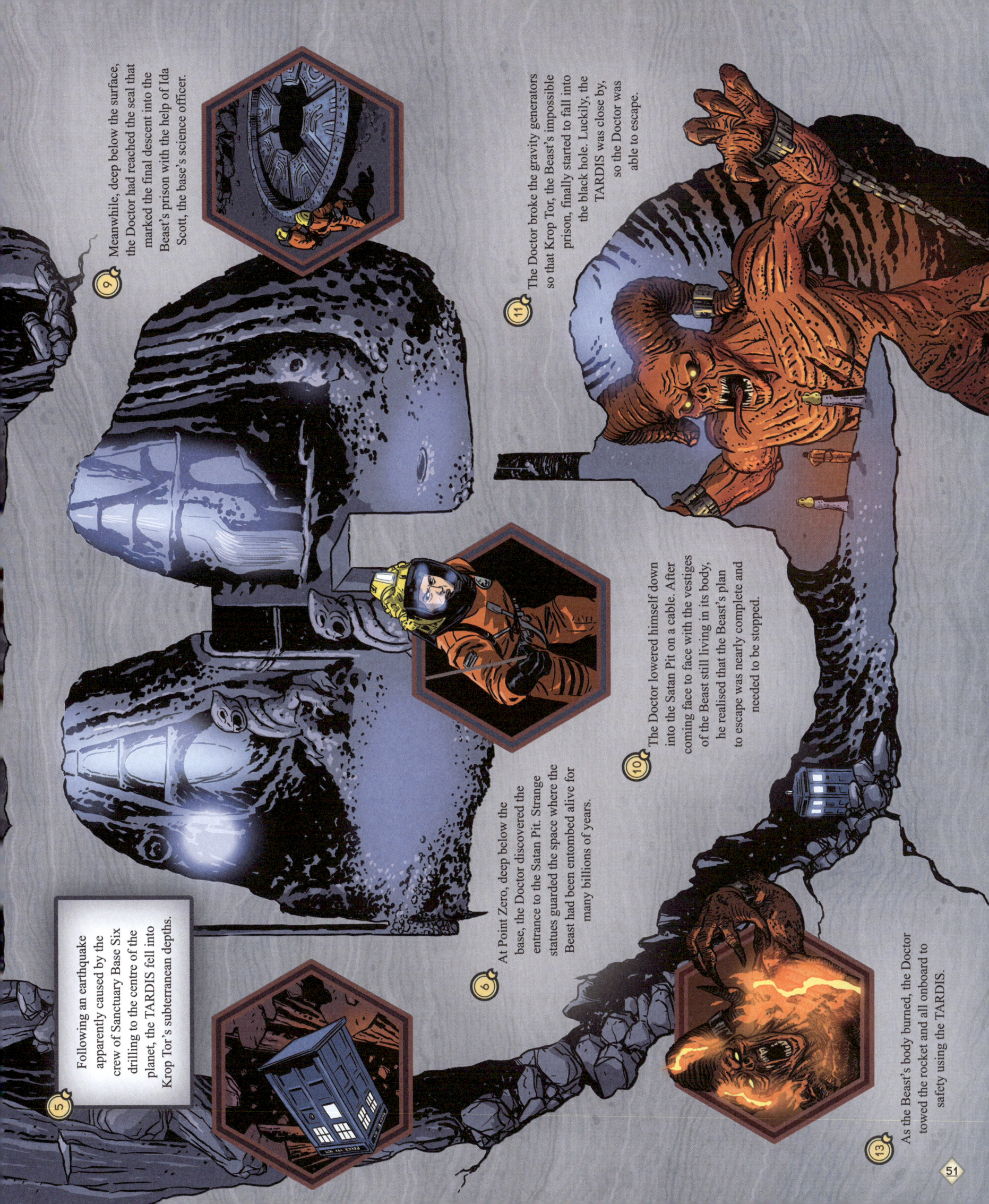

5 Following an earthquake apparently caused by the crew of Sanctuary Base Six drilling to the centre of the planet, the TARDIS fell into Krop Tor's subterranean depths.

9 Meanwhile, deep below the surface, the Doctor had reached the final descent into the Beast's prison with the help of Ida Scott, the base's science officer.

11 The Doctor broke the gravity generators so that Krop Tor, the Beast's impossible prison, finally started to fall into the black hole. Luckily, the TARDIS was close by, so the Doctor was able to escape.

6 At Point Zero, deep below the base, the Doctor discovered the entrance to the Satan Pit. Strange statues guarded the space where the Beast had been entombed alive for many billions of years.

10 The Doctor lowered himself down into the Satan Pit on a cable. After coming face to face with the vestiges of the Beast still living in its body, he realised that the Beast's plan to escape was nearly complete and needed to be stopped.

13 As the Beast's body burned, the Doctor towed the rocket and all onboard to safety using the TARDIS.

SATELLITE FIVE / THE GAME STATION

The Ninth Doctor visited this vast space station in two different time periods. In the year 200,000 it was called Satellite Five, the broadcast centre of Earth's news service. A hundred years later it had become known as the Game Station, and was now transmitting numerous game shows across the Earth. In both eras, however, the Doctor discovered that those controlling the space station were manipulating humanity for their own ends.

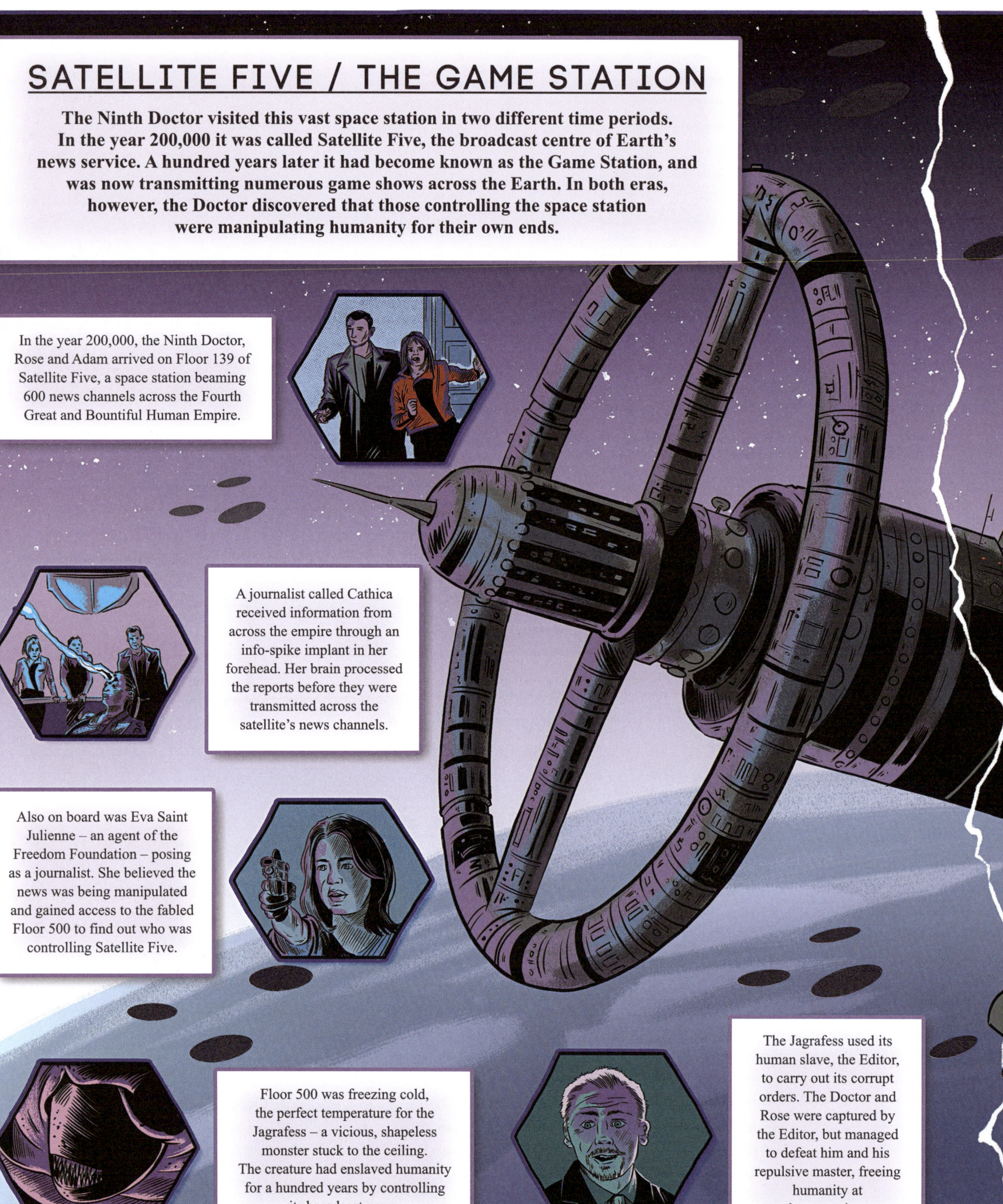

In the year 200,000, the Ninth Doctor, Rose and Adam arrived on Floor 139 of Satellite Five, a space station beaming 600 news channels across the Fourth Great and Bountiful Human Empire.

A journalist called Cathica received information from across the empire through an info-spike implant in her forehead. Her brain processed the reports before they were transmitted across the satellite's news channels.

Also on board was Eva Saint Julienne – an agent of the Freedom Foundation – posing as a journalist. She believed the news was being manipulated and gained access to the fabled Floor 500 to find out who was controlling Satellite Five.

Floor 500 was freezing cold, the perfect temperature for the Jagrafess – a vicious, shapeless monster stuck to the ceiling. The creature had enslaved humanity for a hundred years by controlling its broadcast news.

The Jagrafess used its human slave, the Editor, to carry out its corrupt orders. The Doctor and Rose were captured by the Editor, but managed to defeat him and his repulsive master, freeing humanity at the same time.

 In the year 200,100, the TARDIS was intercepted and the Doctor found himself on the TV show, *Big Brother*! He was actually back on board Satellite Five – now called the Game Station – which beamed deadly game shows across the Earth.

 In another studio, the Doctor's friend Captain Jack was trapped in a makeover show hosted by two robots – Trine-E and Zu-Zana. They planned to give him a full-body makeover by subjecting him to brutal cosmetic surgery. Luckily, he destroyed them first.

 On Floor 500, the Doctor discovered a fleet of Dalek ships heading for the Game Station. The Daleks had been manipulating humanity and its systems for centuries, and were also responsible for installing the Jagrafess.

 Elsewhere, the Anne Droid hosted another deadly game show, *The Weakest Link*. When contestants were voted off, the robot appeared to incinerate them using a powerful laser – but in fact they were transported to a Dalek spaceship.

 The Emperor Dalek gloated that his Daleks had been harvesting genetic material from humans kidnapped from the Game Station. As a result, they had now created a huge Dalek army impossible to resist . . .

When Rose looked into the heart of the TARDIS, the time vortex itself began to flow through her head, giving her incredible, god-like powers. She succeeded in destroying the Emperor and his entire fleet of Dalek ships.

 To save Rose from the lethal power of the time vortex, the Doctor channelled it away from her, but in doing so he destroyed all the cells in his body. To survive, he was forced to regenerate into a brand-new body . . .

TITANIC SPACE LINER

Once there was an ill-fated ship on Earth named the *RMS Titanic* that sank on its first voyage. Almost one hundred years later, the Tenth Doctor landed on a luxury cruise liner with the same name from the planet Sto, and it too met with disaster.

6 High above the engines was the engine deck – a high-tech chasm crossable only by a narrow bridge of nitrofin metal. Here, the Doctor's group was attacked by the Host, but cyborg Bannakaffalatta sacrificed himself to save them.

Public viewing decks and promenade corridors allowed passengers to gaze out at passing planets and marvel at the enormity of space.

9 Brave waitress Astrid Peth saved the Doctor by using a forklift truck to hurl the *Titanic*'s evil owner into the ship's engines – at the cost of her own life.

The *Titanic*'s dining area and ballroom was a vast, luxurious space for passengers, complete with an enormous Christmas tree to mark the festive voyage.

5 On Deck 22, the Doctor realised that the meteor impact had left the *Titanic* on a crash-course with Earth. Along with a group of survivors, he set off on an attempt to reach the bridge and regain control of the ship.

The *Titanic* was powered by nuclear storm engines in the base of the ship. But after the disaster they were cycling down and on the verge of failing.

3 Deck 31 was the storage deck for the *Titanic*'s robot servants, the 'Heavenly Host'. A technical malfunction caused them to turn hostile, and they began to slaughter passengers all over the spaceship.

8 The creature who doomed the *Titanic* was its owner, Max Capricorn. He wanted the ship to crash on Earth so its engines would wipe out all life – while he hid in an impact chamber to survive.

1. The *Titanic* was controlled from the bridge, situated at the bow of the ship. Modern tech sat alongside an old ship's wheel connected to sensitive space sensors.

2. Captain Hardaker, who was dying from a terminal illness, took a bribe to help his family financially by destroying the ship. As a meteoroid shower approached from portside, he deliberately lowered the *Titanic*'s safety shields and was killed in the collision (along with most most of his passengers and crew).

4. There were many kitchens on board the *Titanic* to feed the vast number of passengers. After the ship's disastrous collision, the only surviving galley staff hid in Kitchen 5 but were eliminated by the reprogrammed Host robots.

The logo for Max Capricorn's failing company. Kicked out by the other board members, Max wanted to frame them for the *Titanic* disaster while he retired happily to Penhaxico Two.

10. It was down to the Doctor to stop the *Titanic* crashing into Earth – and it barely missed Buckingham Palace! The heat of entering the planet's atmosphere fired up the secondary storm drive, saving the stricken ship.

7. In Kitchen 3, the Doctor exploited loopholes in the Host's programming in order to trick them into taking him to the mastermind behind the disaster.

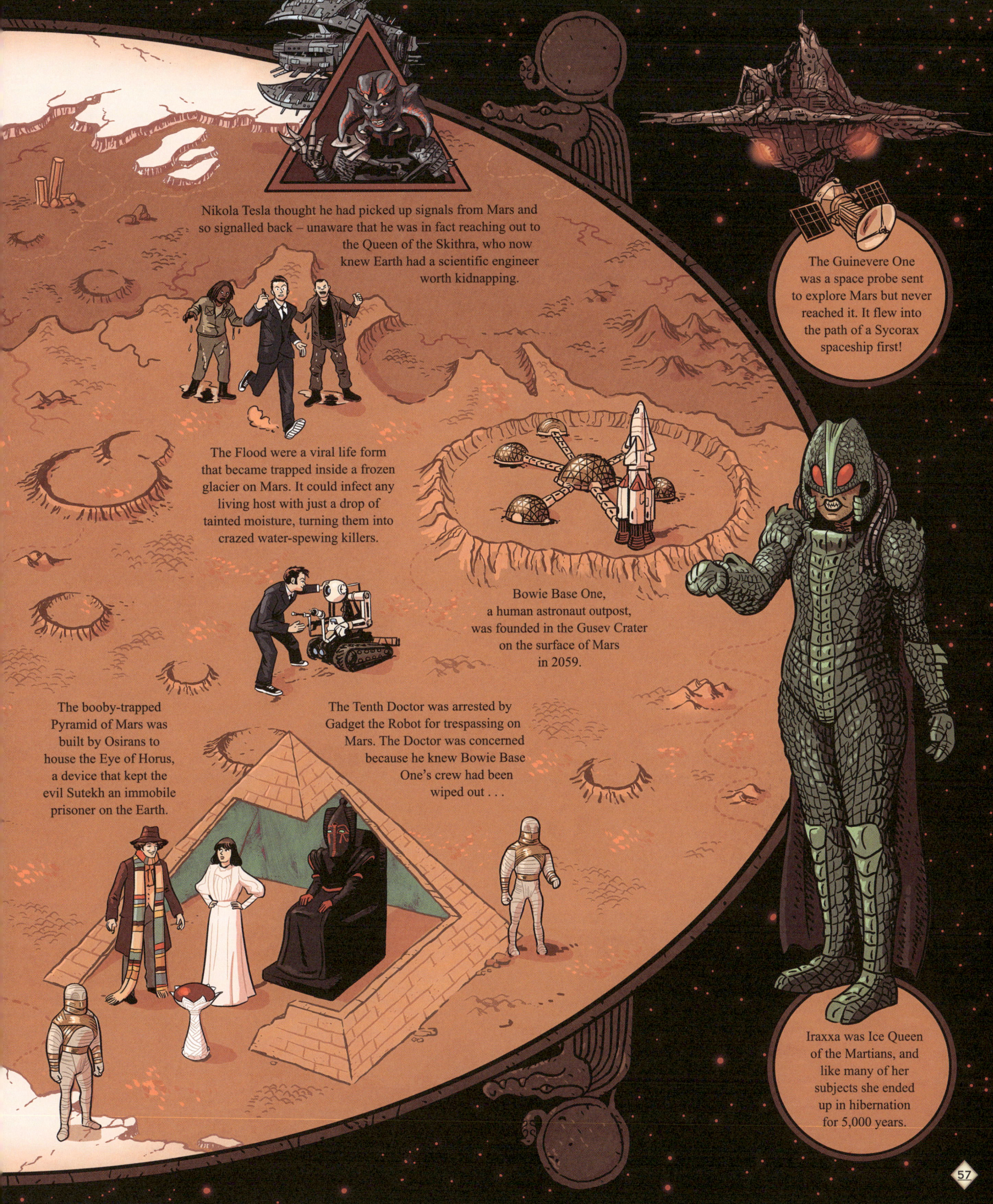

THE MOON

The Moon is our satellite. Orbiting at an average distance of 238,857 miles, it is Earth's nearest neighbour in space. It has been a launch pad for human space exploration and has been visited by many alien aggressors over the years!

In 2070, Earth's weather was controlled from an international moonbase using a Gravitron machine to send gravitational waves into the atmosphere.

When the Cybermen tried to take control of the moonbase, the Second Doctor was able to deflect their invasion fleet into space using the power of the Gravitron.

The Third Doctor was locked up on the Moon. His escape attempts failed every time – until the evil Master 'rescued' him, and then his troubles really started!

In the late twenty-first century, another Moonbase controlled the T-Mat instant-travel system used to transport food and people all over Earth. It was taken over by Ice Warriors and used to deliver deadly seed pods all over our world.

The Lunar Penal Colony is a human prison colony located on the Moon. Political prisoners are often sent here after being handed life sentences.

The Second Doctor was able to defeat the Martian invaders with powerful heatlamps, which reduced Ice Warriors into a puddle of slime!

MARINUS

When the First Doctor and his companions Ian, Barbara and Susan landed on the planet Marinus, they found a beach of glass beside an acid sea. These were only the first of many dangers they encountered as they searched the strange planet for a very special set of keys . . .

9 Ian and Barbara found themselves transported to a snowy wasteland. After an encounter with the treacherous Vasor, they were reunited with Susan and soon located the fourth key inside a block of ice. However, when the travellers used heat from a volcanic spring to melt the ice, they also reanimated the deadly Ice Soldiers who guarded the key. They barely escaped with their lives from the battle that followed, but now had four keys in their possession.

2 Arbitan only had the first key, but he needed the others to reactivate the Conscience, which had been upgraded to resist Voord interference. Arbitan persuaded the Doctor and his companions to find the other keys for him using instant-travel dials.

10 Finally, the Doctor had to expose a murderer in the courts of the city of Millennius to save Ian from a death sentence and locate the fifth key, which was hidden inside the murder weapon.

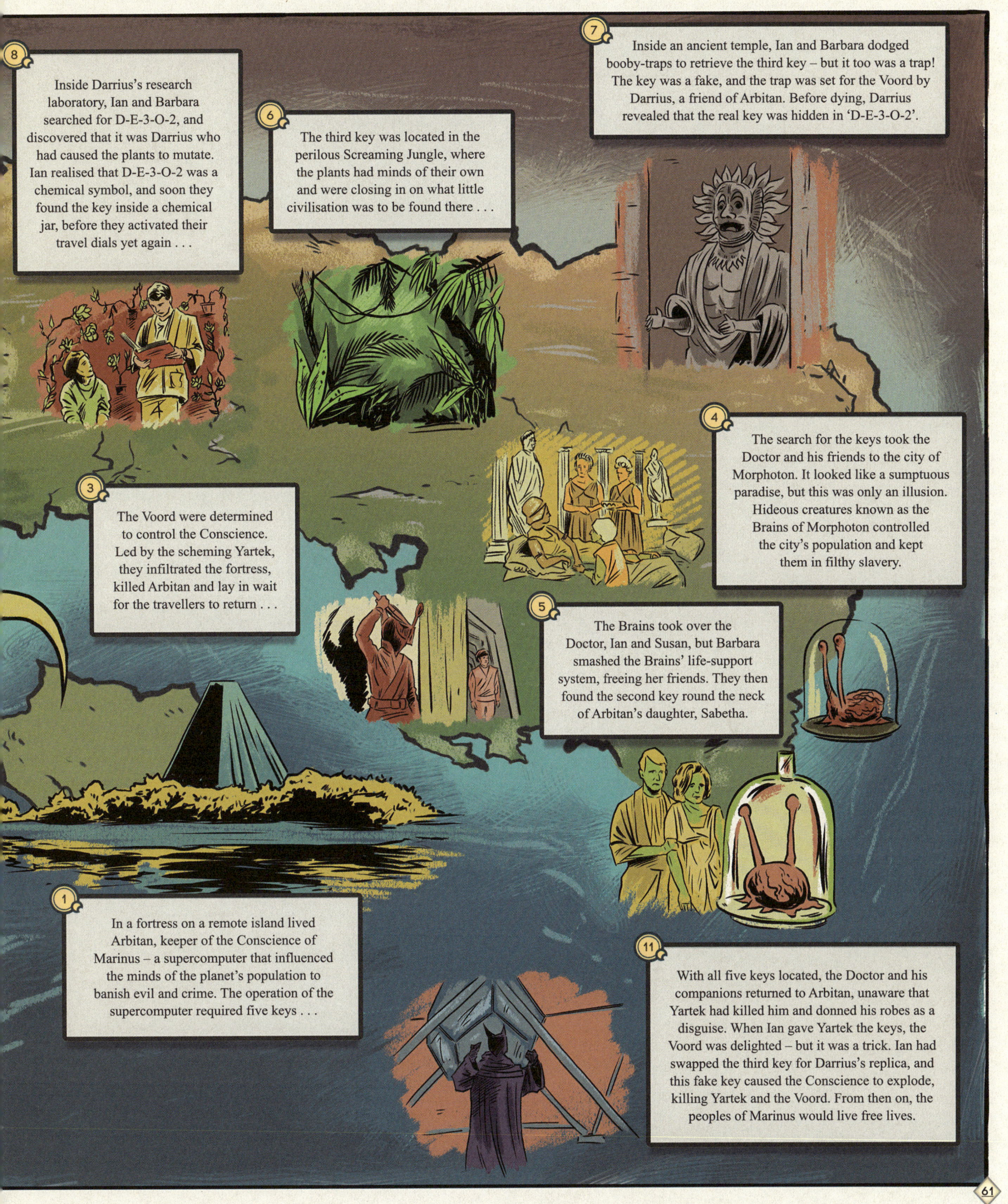

THE MEDUSA CASCADE

Halfway across the universe from Earth lies the Medusa Cascade. This colourful, gaseous region was once the site of a rift in space and time that was sealed by the Doctor. Davros, together with his New Dalek Empire, transported twenty-seven planetary bodies here and hid them in a time pocket, ready to fulfil his plan to use their energy patterns to activate a reality bomb. In doing so, he intended to destroy everything in known existence.

The fiery planet of Pyrovillia – home of the Pyroviles – was also taken.

The planet Adipose 3 – home of the Adipose – was among the worlds taken.

The Adipose are creatures formed almost entirely of fat. Matron Cofelia, an overzealous Adipose nanny, broke galactic law by breeding Adipose on Earth after the Adipose breeding world was lost. Using special diet pills, Adipose Industries grew the Adipose inside living human bodies!

The Pyroviles are creatures of stone and magma. When Pyrovillia was stolen, some Pyroviles escaped to Earth, plotting to turn it into a new home world and transforming humans into Pyroviles as they went. Little did they know, the Earth would one day be stolen too!

The TARDIS ultimately towed all the stolen planets back to their correct time–space locations across the universe.

Shallacatop was another planet stolen to help give power to the reality bomb.

The lost moon of Poosh was among the worlds taken – a fact the Doctor learned by chance while visiting the planet Midnight.

The uninhabited Callufrax Minor was placed among the stolen planets.

Also taken was the planet of Woman Wept, which has a continent shaped like a lamenting woman. After a catastrophic solar event, the planet's entire ocean froze over in an instant, leaving vast icy waves and tsunamis standing like mountains.

Jahoo was another uninhabited world stolen by the Daleks.

The identities of the other planets remain unknown for now . . .

The Earth was stolen in 2009, and was the final world needed to power Davros's reality bomb.

The world of Griffoth – home to the mischievous puzzle-loving Graske – was among the twenty-seven worlds removed from their position in time and space.

Davros, creator of the Daleks and founder of the New Dalek Empire, devised the reality bomb. It could destroy all forms of life throughout this universe and any other – except for Dalek life, which was to be held safely in the eye of the storm.

Clom, the sister world of Raxacoricofallapatorius and home to the life-absorbing Abzorbaloff, was also taken.

The Supreme Dalek oversaw this vast plot to destroy all creation from the Crucible, a massive Dalek space station from which the reality bomb would be deployed.

STARSHIP UK

When Earth's safety was threatened by solar flares in the twenty-ninth century, its people headed out to space to search for a new home. The United Kingdom was one of the last countries to leave Earth, and it did so with a 'starship' unlike any other, where millions lived in a strangely governed society in which whole counties had been turned into buildings.

2 Winders kept the machinery of the starship going. They watched the population to check the rules were being followed.

5 When he arrived on Starship UK, the Eleventh Doctor used a glass of water to show Amy that something was amiss with how the starship was being powered. After all, if there were no vibrations from the engines, how were they moving through space?

1 The population of Starship UK made decisions about the ship's future using voting booths. Here, they were shown the truth about how the ship was powered, with the option to 'forget' or 'protest'. However, they were warned that if even one per cent of the population chose 'protest', there would be huge repercussions for them all.

9 Liz Ten aimed to take back control of her starship by turning on the Smilers and helping the Doctor.

People used special lifts – or 'vators – to navigate the many levels of Starship UK.

3 The Smilers promoted good behaviour. If a Smiler stopped smiling, you were in trouble!

4 The ruler of Starship UK was Liz Ten – the far-future Queen of the UK. She didn't seem to know quite what was happening under the surface of her own realm.

8 Instead of encountering a terrifying beast, Liz Ten learned the truth about Starship UK – it was not powered by an engine, but by the last Star Whale. It had come to Earth wishing to help the stranded population of the UK, but in their fear they had enslaved and tortured it into taking them out into space. Liz Ten had a choice – abdicate and set the whale free, or continue to reign and keep Starship UK safe.

7 The Winders – who were secretly half-Smilers – were not happy with their monarch. She was taken to learn the truth of the beast below . . .

10 When the Doctor discovered the truth about how the Star Whale was treated, he was furious. But, after seeing the Star Whale playing with children, Amy realised that it was carrying Starship UK out of kindness.

6 The Doctor and Amy angered the Smilers and the Winders in their search for answers. They were thrown down a chute to a murky underworld level . . .

11 Amy convinced Liz Ten to abdicate, but, despite all the pain that it had endured, the Star Whale continued to carry Starship UK through the universe of its own free will.

12 Happy now that the Star Whale was no longer being used so cruelly, Liz Ten promised to make her starship a happier, less secretive place from then on.

65

ALFAVA METRAXIS

Alfava Metraxis is the seventh planet in the Dundra System, in the Garn Belt. Originally home to the Aplan civilisation – who mysteriously died out – the planet was terraformed and colonised by billions of humans by the fifty-first century. Little did the humans realise, they were sharing their planet with a deadly force of Weeping Angels . . .

1 Weeping Angels hunted the two-headed Aplans to extinction. Without a power source, they lay dormant and decaying in an underground Aplan mortarium – a labyrinth of tombs full of disintegrating statues of the dead.

2 The Eleventh Doctor and Amy were drawn to Alfava Metraxis when River Song led them to the home box (like an aircraft's black box) of the spaceship *Byzantium*.

3 The *Byzantium* was carrying a Weeping Angel when it crashed through the roof of the Aplan mortarium. The Angel escaped.

10 The Angels gloated that one of their kind was forming inside Amy; having got into her eyes, it was taking control of her mind. Amy had to keep her eyes closed – the second she opened them, it would emerge and kill her.

11 The Angels noticed that a mysterious crack in time had opened on the ship. The Doctor realised it was leaking pure time energy and anyone touched by the light would be erased from existence.

12 After becoming separated from the Doctor and River, Amy had to pretend that she could see in order to fool the roaming Angels into standing still when she approached. The Angels weren't fooled for long, but Amy was teleported to safety by River.

13 The Doctor finally defeated the Angels when the artificial gravity in the *Byzantium* switched off and the Angels tumbled through the crack in time, writing themselves out of existence – and freeing Amy from their hold.

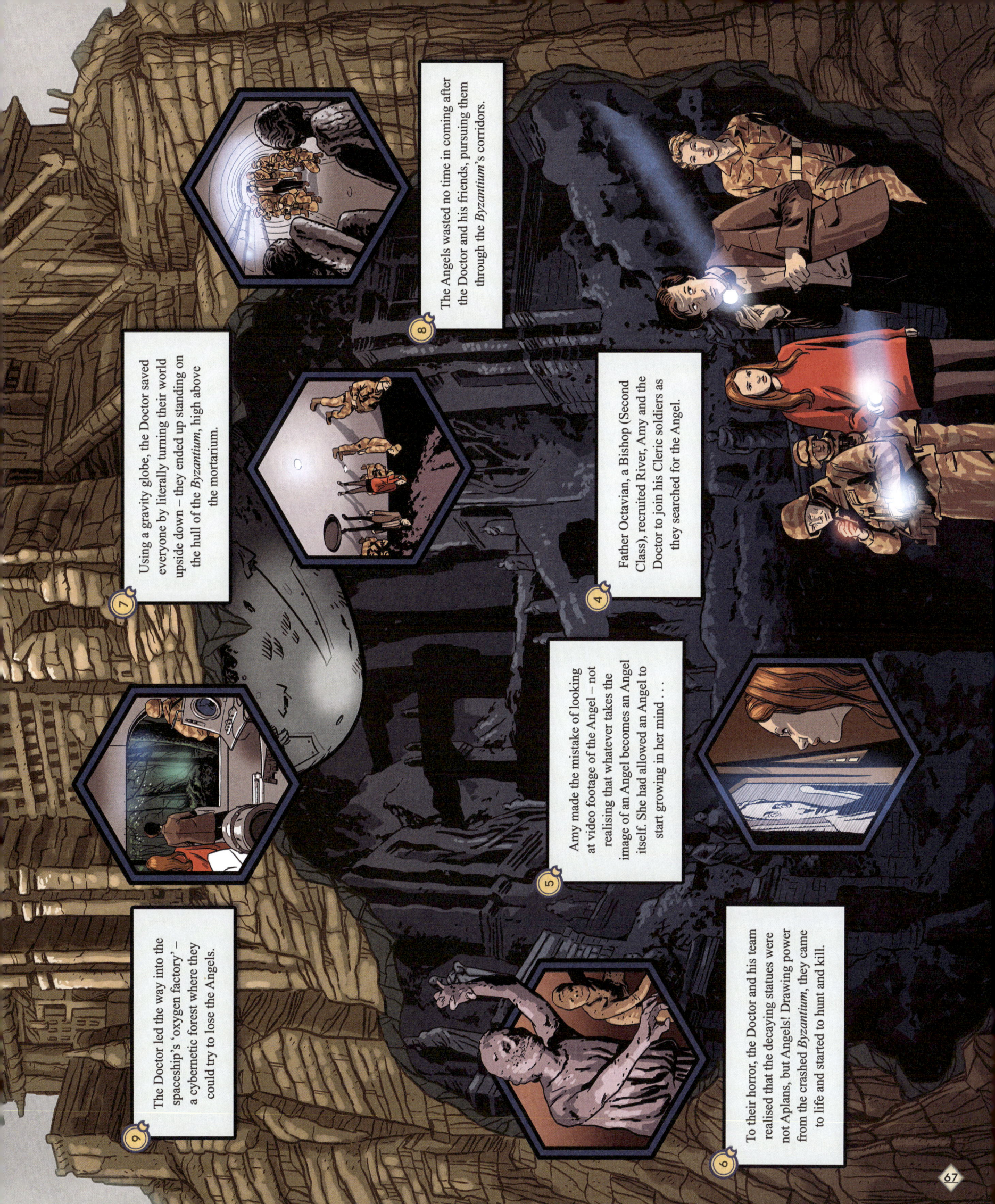

4. Father Octavian, a Bishop (Second Class), recruited River, Amy and the Doctor to join his Cleric soldiers as they searched for the Angel.

5. Amy made the mistake of looking at video footage of the Angel – not realising that whatever takes the image of an Angel becomes an Angel itself. She had allowed an Angel to start growing in her mind . . .

6. To their horror, the Doctor and his team realised that the decaying statues were not Aplans, but Angels! Drawing power from the crashed *Byzantium*, they came to life and started to hunt and kill.

7. Using a gravity globe, the Doctor saved everyone by literally turning their world upside down – they ended up standing on the hull of the *Byzantium*, high above the mortarium.

8. The Angels wasted no time in coming after the Doctor and his friends, pursuing them through the *Byzantium*'s corridors.

9. The Doctor led the way into the spaceship's 'oxygen factory' – a cybernetic forest where they could try to lose the Angels.

67

TRENZALORE

On the planet Trenzalore lies the town of Christmas, which the Doctor once spent 900 years defending: a sleepy, snowy little community with a crack in time hidden in the clock tower. The Time Lords, trapped in a pocket dimension, sought to return to our universe through the crack by asking a single question over and over: 'Doctor who?' If the Doctor confirmed his real name, the Time Lords would know they were in the right place. Ominously, Trenzalore was also said to be the Doctor's final resting place – the world on which he finally died.

Tasha Lem, Mother Superious of the Church of the Papal Mainframe, worked with the Silence to protect Trenzalore from destruction and ensure the Time Lords did not return to restart the Time War.

The siege dragged on for 900 years, until ultimately the Time Lords chose not to return. They granted the Doctor a whole new regeneration cycle, infusing him with enough power to destroy the Dalek warfleet.

The evil, snake-like Mara manifested from the dark void beyond the mind, intent on ending the Time Lords' power to return to the universe.

The plastic Autons were sent into combat in Christmas by the Nestene Consciousness.

The reptilian Ice Warriors and deadly plant-creatures the Krynoids also attempted to break the Siege of Trenzalore.

Sontarans tried to enter using an invisibility shield – but this subterfuge was seen through!

Everyone aboard the space church was eventually killed by the Daleks and turned into their puppets, tricking and almost killing the Eleventh Doctor and Clara. Only Tasha Lem was strong enough to reassert her own will.

Alien warfleets gathered around Trenzalore, ready to destroy it. The return of the Time Lords would reignite the Time War that laid waste to the universe, and they sought to destroy the entry point before that could happen . . .

Technology could be detected by the Church, so alien invaders had to be inventive. A design of a wooden Cyberman was created to infiltrate Christmas, but the Doctor stopped it.

The Doctor was kept company in Christmas by Handles, a Cyberman head cleaned out and converted into a literal-minded robot. Handles saved the Doctor's life many times.

Before the Church of the Papal Mainframe put a protective forcefield around Trenzalore, Weeping Angels hid themselves in the snowdrifts around Christmas.

The Great Intelligence and the Whisper Men brought the Doctor to his own tomb in order to gain access to his time stream. By entering it, the Great Intelligence hoped to turn all of the Doctor's victories into defeats, until Clara foiled its plans.

In an alternate timeline, the Doctor died defending Trenzalore and his TARDIS became his tomb. Due to a size leak, it expanded into a giant ruin.

There was no body inside the TARDIS tomb – only the Doctor's time stream; a vast open wound running through reality.

69

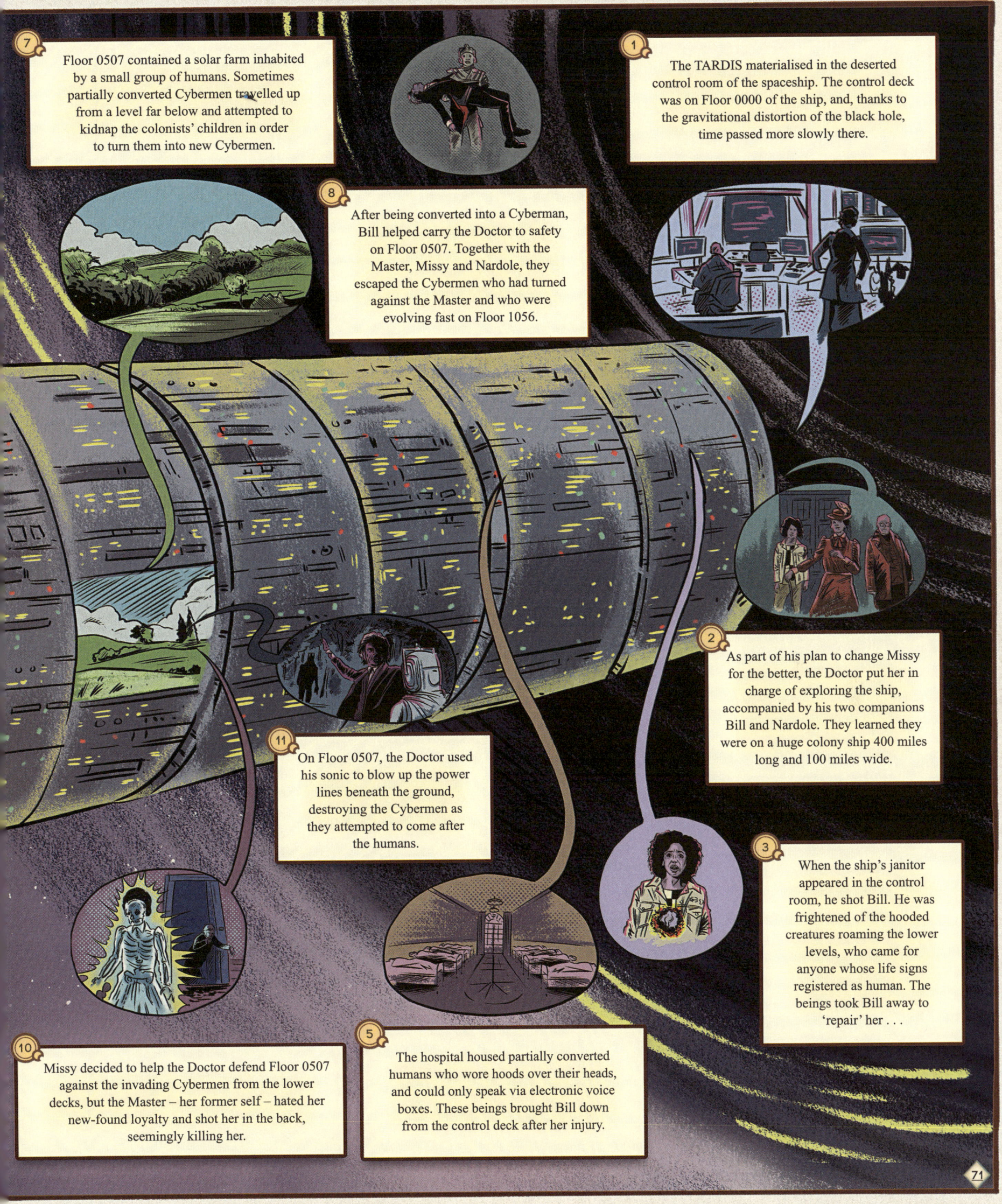

CONFESSION DIAL

A confession dial is a piece of Gallifreyan technology. Dying Time Lords use them to make peace with themselves before their minds are uploaded to the Matrix to add to the sum total of Time Lord experience and knowledge. However, a confession dial can be converted to become a terrifying prison for its owner. This happened to the Twelfth Doctor, who was trapped within his own confession dial and forced to live out the same disturbing sequence of events over and over again for 4.5 billion years . . .

He burned up his body to provide power for the teleport pod. A new copy of the Doctor's unharmed self stepped out, but not before his previous self had the chance to scrawl the word 'BIRD' in the dust on the floor . . .

Refusing to die, the Doctor forced himself to crawl back up countless stairs, desperate to reach the teleport chamber and save himself.

The Doctor eventually found room twelve, which contained a wall of ultra-hard Azbantium labelled 'HOME'. He started punching his way through the wall, like the bird pecking away at the mountain, but he was caught and injured by the creature.

After walking up to the castle ramparts, the Doctor realised the stars were in the wrong position and deduced that he'd been a prisoner in the castle for an incredibly long time.

Back in the teleport chamber where he first arrived, the Doctor found another human skull and another cryptic clue – the word 'BIRD' traced in the dust. Staring at the clue, he remembered a story about a bird that pecked at a diamond mountain for billions of years . . .

Venturing outside again, the Doctor found a spade and a patch of earth. He started digging for more clues and eventually uncovered the words 'I am in 12' etched on to a stone slab.

The Doctor stepped out of a teleport pod into an empty stone chamber. He noticed a pile of dust on the floor and wondered what it was.

Edging down a deserted corridor, the Doctor peered out of the window and realised he was trapped inside an enormous castle surrounded by water.

Unbeknown to the Doctor, a nightmare creature from his childhood started to stalk him through the corridors. When he was cornered next to a locked door, the Doctor realised that he could halt the creature in its tracks by confessing a secret.

The walls and ramparts of the castle suddenly shifted position and the locked door opened to reveal a bedchamber. On the wall was an old oil painting of the Doctor's recently departed companion, Clara.

The creature suddenly lurched back into life, and, desperate to escape his relentless pursuer, the Doctor broke a window and hurled himself out of it.

Diving into the water below, the Doctor discovered hundreds of ancient human skulls – it seemed he was not the first to become trapped in the castle.

Back inside, the Doctor was surprised to find a roaring fire and an identical change of clothes waiting for him in one of the great halls.

Finally, after billions of years, the Doctor broke through the Azbantium wall. The creature and his prison were revealed to be mechanical components in his confession dial on his home planet of Gallifrey – and the Doctor vowed to make those Time Lords responsible for his imprisonment pay!

DESOLATION

Usually marked only with a warning symbol, Desolation is the closest thing to a name given to the final planet in the Rally of the Twelve Galaxies – a race with over 4,000 competitors and a prize of 3.2 trillion krin. The planet was 'created cruel', with deadly water, a toxic atmosphere and many different terrains. It was also the location of the mysterious Ghost Monument . . .

1. Epzo, a Muxteran pilot, was one of the final two competitors in the rally, and he was desperate for the prize money. His ship, the Cerebos, crash-landed on Desolation.

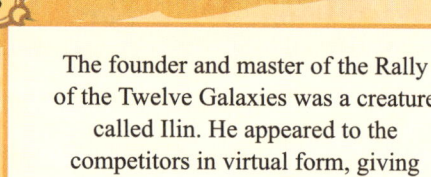
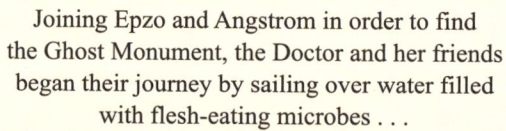

2. Epzo's final opponent, Angstrom, was from the planet Albar. She wanted to use the prize money to save her family from evil Stenza invaders.

3. The founder and master of the Rally of the Twelve Galaxies was a creature called Ilin. He appeared to the competitors in virtual form, giving information and setting terms.

5. Joining Epzo and Angstrom in order to find the Ghost Monument, the Doctor and her friends began their journey by sailing over water filled with flesh-eating microbes . . .

4. Ilin showed the Thirteenth Doctor and her friends the Ghost Monument that haunted Desolation . . . it was the TARDIS, which the Doctor had thought lost!

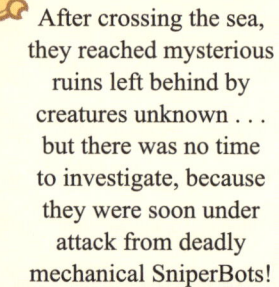
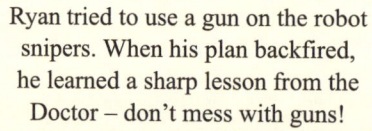

6. After crossing the sea, they reached mysterious ruins left behind by creatures unknown . . . but there was no time to investigate, because they were soon under attack from deadly mechanical SniperBots!

7. Ryan tried to use a gun on the robot snipers. When his plan backfired, he learned a sharp lesson from the Doctor – don't mess with guns!

ORPHAN 55

When a planet is graded as an 'orphan', it indicates that the environment has become too toxic to support life. Orphan 55 started out abundant in flora and fauna, but pollution and global warming took their toll. When the Thirteenth Doctor, Ryan, Graham and Yaz visited Orphan 55, they found that in one possible timeline it used to have a different name – it was known as Earth . . .

3 Hideous creatures known as Dregs broke into Tranquillity Spa and began to attack the guests. The Dregs were savage creatures that had adapted to the environmental changes of Orphan 55 and possessed telepathic powers.

2 In reality, the spa was a 'fakation' resort, housed within a survival dome located in post-apocalyptic Siberia on Orphan 55. The tropical scenery was created by advanced hologram projectors and protected by an ionic membrane.

4 The Doctor, Yaz, Ryan and Graham discovered the truth about Tranquillity Spa when a hole developed in the ionic membrane, revealing the barren world beyond.

8 The rescue team escaped through the bottom of the truck and barely made it to the tunnels leading back to Tranquillity Spa. The Doctor noticed that all the signs were written in Russian, leading her to realise that Orphan 55 was, in fact, Earth.

11 The only way to escape the Dregs was to use a teleport station to leave Orphan 55 – but it had broken down.

9 The Doctor and Yaz helped Kane (who had been injured) to make the journey as Vilma sacrificed herself to buy them time. But danger was closer than they thought – Kane's estranged daughter, Bella, was planning to blow up Tranquillity Spa, and the tunnel they were in led straight through a Dreg nest . . .

10 When the Doctor encountered the Dreg leader, she contacted them telepathically. After seeing visions of twenty-first-century Earth in crisis, she realised that the Dregs were mutated humans who had been forced to evolve after their destructive behaviour and greed had wrecked the planet's ecosystems.

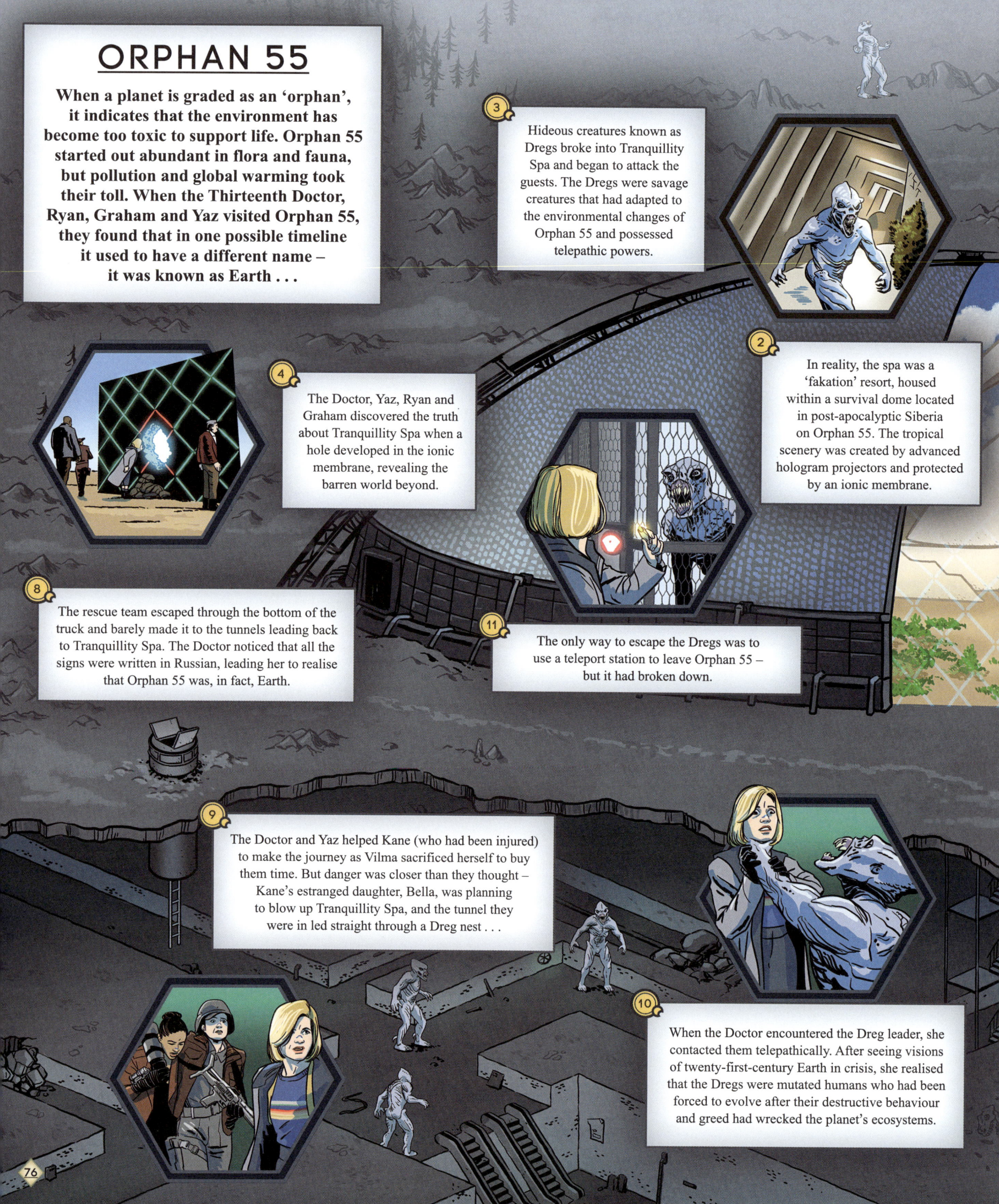

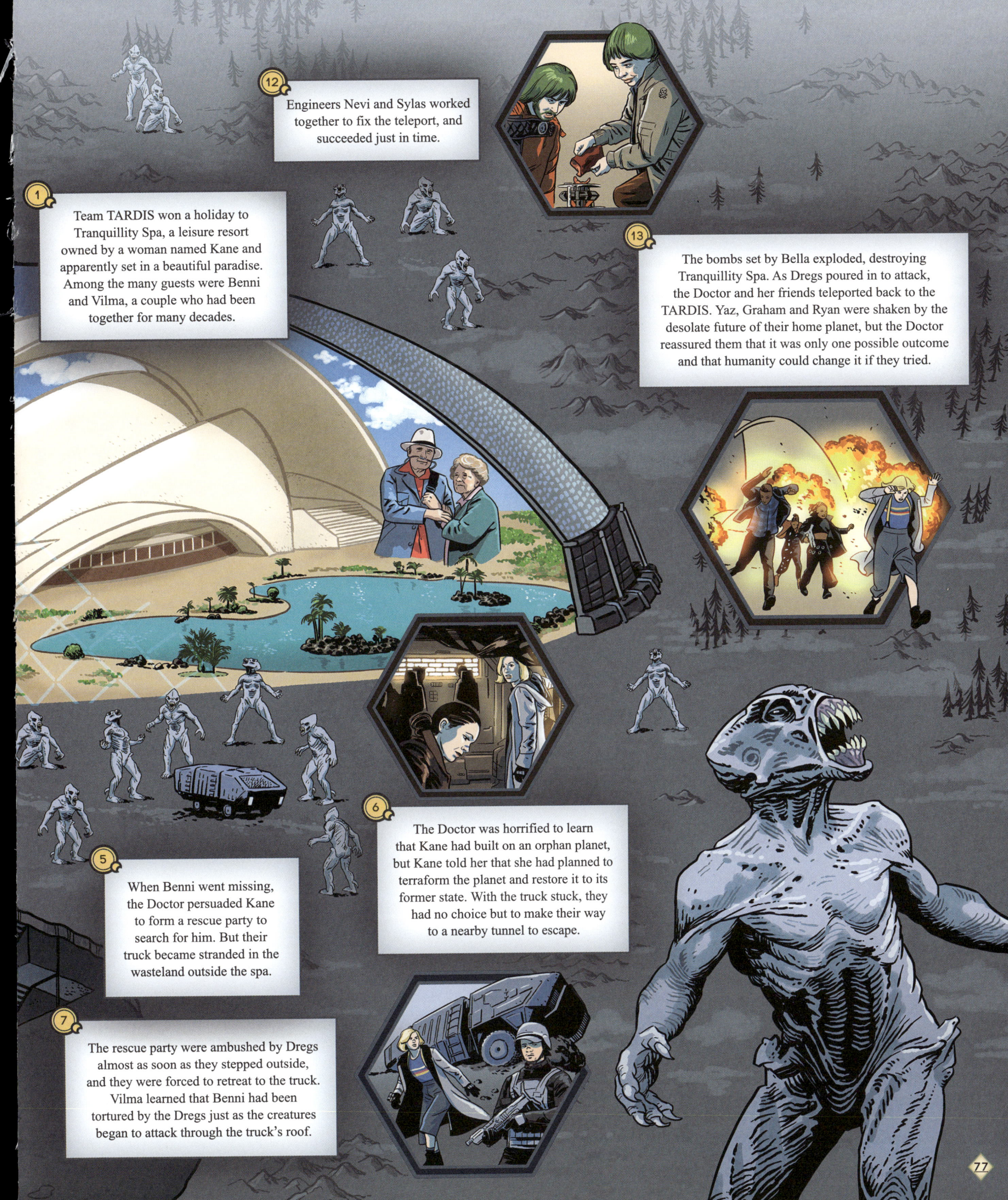

12 Engineers Nevi and Sylas worked together to fix the teleport, and succeeded just in time.

1 Team TARDIS won a holiday to Tranquillity Spa, a leisure resort owned by a woman named Kane and apparently set in a beautiful paradise. Among the many guests were Benni and Vilma, a couple who had been together for many decades.

13 The bombs set by Bella exploded, destroying Tranquillity Spa. As Dregs poured in to attack, the Doctor and her friends teleported back to the TARDIS. Yaz, Graham and Ryan were shaken by the desolate future of their home planet, but the Doctor reassured them that it was only one possible outcome and that humanity could change it if they tried.

6 The Doctor was horrified to learn that Kane had built on an orphan planet, but Kane told her that she had planned to terraform the planet and restore it to its former state. With the truck stuck, they had no choice but to make their way to a nearby tunnel to escape.

5 When Benni went missing, the Doctor persuaded Kane to form a rescue party to search for him. But their truck became stranded in the wasteland outside the spa.

7 The rescue party were ambushed by Dregs almost as soon as they stepped outside, and they were forced to retreat to the truck. Vilma learned that Benni had been tortured by the Dregs just as the creatures began to attack through the truck's roof.